W9-BXE-393

THIS
IS FOR
TONIGHT

THIS
IS FOR
TONIGHT

Jessica Patrick

READS

NEW YORK

A Swoon Reads Book
An imprint of Feiwel and Friends and Macmillan Publishing Group, LLC
120 Broadway, New York, NY 10271
swoonreads.com

Library of Congress Control Number: 2020919828
First edition, 2021
Book design by Mallory Grigg
Printed in the United States of America
ISBN 9781250757159 (hardcover)
10 9 8 7 6 5 4 3 2 1

To my parents, who taught me
to love books and music

››› • ‹‹‹

CHAPTER 1

>>> • <<<

"AND DON'T FORGET TO LIKE AND SUBSCRI—"

My twin brother barges into my bedroom right as I'm filming the closing for my latest YouTube video. Delicate flower that he is, he slams the door behind him, causing my desk to shake, which in turn topples my delicately rigged ring light. The light falls onto my tripod, knocking my vlog camera from its precarious spot on my desk right into the trash can. *Bonk-clank-plop.* It's like the old game Mouse Trap, but with semiexpensive electronics.

"And one," Jordan says, making some kind of basketball motion with his hands.

"Damn it, you ass, I was filming. I finally got a take without my voice doing that scratchy thing, and you ruined it." The only projectile I have to fling at him is the friendship bracelet I made for today's video, but it's so light it just floats limply to the carpet.

"Sorry 'bout that." Jordan flops onto my bed and starfishes out. We were the same height until about seventh grade, but then he shot up like a rocket, cementing his destiny as a basketball star, and I stayed the same shrimpy height. So, while I can actually spread myself out on my twin bed with room to spare, Jordan's long legs dangle over the end and his large hands graze the carpet. "And sorry I'm late."

"You're always late," I say, stretching my leg out to kick his dangling arm. "And you're never sorry."

"I have awesome news to make up for it, though."

"To make up for thirty entire minutes? It better be good. You said you'd help me today, Jordan. Luckily I had other parts of this video I could film while I was waiting for your slow ass, but you even ruined that." I hop up from behind the second desk in my room, a small garage sale Ikea piece I painted hot pink to use as a video set, and I fish my camera and tripod out of the trash can. "You owe me some In-N-Out."

"Add it to my tab." Jordan sits up quickly, scoots toward the end of the bed, and rests his elbows on his knees. "So, do you want to hear this news or what?"

I grab one of the throw pillows from my bed, a purple one that I hand-beaded for a video last month, and I smack him in the head with it. "The only thing I want to hear is the sound of you making friendship bracelets with me for the next hour or so for this video. And not laughing at your own jokes in the middle of every take like last time. That's it."

"But, Andi, this is—"

"Jordan, you promised. You're my only option right now. Plus, you took the car with my ring light in the back the other day when I told you I needed it. And you ate the last of the cereal yesterday. You owe me, dude." My hands flex in and out of fists as I try to keep myself from losing it on my brother. "I promise I'll listen to whatever you want to tell me as soon as you let me walk you through the intricate steps of friendship bracelet design with your smile on and your mouth shut. Got it?"

Jordan smirks and lowers himself onto one knee, then bends forward into an elaborate bow. "I am at your service."

"Good. Now, this is my final product." I grab the friendship bracelet I tried to throw at him and wave it in his face. I made it last night while binge-watching cake-decorating videos, and it turned out pretty close to perfect. "I'm going to walk through the directions for one of these bad boys, but I'm going to give alternate, easier directions for a beginner design that's less complicated, and that's the one you're going to do."

"I always get the dumbed-down version."

"It's called offering modifications. Okay, sit. And pick out four colors you want to use from the embroidery floss box while I set up the camera again."

"Ah, friendship bracelets," he says as he pokes through my extensive floss stash. "Nonstop thrilling craft project content. Bound to go viral instantly, thanks to the influential middle school contingent."

"Shut it, jerk. Middle schoolers actually *are* an influential audience. And lots of people love crafting. I may not be viral, but my subscribers are into it." I've been making crafting videos for YouTube for about a year now, a total labor of love, and I've developed a small but passionate group of followers. "And who cares about going viral, anyway? Sure, one of these could get picked up and recommended by YouTube and get tons of views and blow my channel up, and believe me, I wouldn't complain. But I'm just here to put out quality content that is useful and interesting. Not be the next *Ryan's World,* or whatever."

Once the camera and light are out of my trash can and back in their places, I head back to my pink desk to sit down and get my own embroidery floss organized. But I can't avoid Jordan's smirk and how he keeps sneaking little peeks at me out of the corner of his eye like he's a cat with a whole mouthful of canary.

"What's up with you?" I ask.

"I told you I had good news. I can't believe you don't want to hear it."

I let out a long, pained sigh. This is so Jordan. He'll be completely insufferable until I let him spill.

"Let me guess. That hot girl from the movie theater finally followed you back? Or you completed the bacon eating challenge at the diner? Is your picture on the wall now? Did you get the 'I'm a Big Pig!' bumper sticker to proudly display?"

"I was trying to tell you that this is good news for you, too." He ties off his purple and gold embroidery floss, LA Lakers colors, clips it on a mini clipboard, and starts knotting himself a friendship bracelet. As much shit as he talks, my brother loves my craft projects, which is why I never have to work hard to convince him to be in my videos. Well, that and the fact that he loves scrolling the comments for people mentioning how hot he is.

I smack his hand. "Save your creativity for filming."

"I think you *are* filming," he says, pointing to the red light on my vlog camera. "It's been recording this whole time."

"Ugh." I get up to turn it off, but he reaches his long arm out to stop me.

"Wait. My news. Let's get this on camera."

"And you say I'm dramatic." I sit back down at my desk, positioning myself right in line with the camera, and speak directly to it like I do when I'm filming a video. "Hi, everyone! Jordan Kennedy, future SCU basketball star and my very favorite twin brother, has some big news. Tell us, Jordan."

Jordan lifts himself off my bed and crowds close to me, putting his face right against mine so we're both in the camera's frame, my hair almost completely blocking his face. "Your boy got two weekend passes plus camping to Cabazon."

My head whips toward him so quickly I'm surprised it doesn't fly right off of my body. "The Cabazon *music festival*?"

"That's the one."

"How did you get those?" The passes for this coming weekend's festival went on sale, and then immediately sold out, months ago. And for the twenty minutes they were available, they cost, like, hundreds of dollars.

"Sergio won them at work." Jordan's best friend works as a valet at a fancy hotel, where he always seems to get nice stuff from people who think it's no big deal. "But he has his grandma's ninetieth birthday party this weekend, so he can't make it."

I stare at him as my brain slowly processes this unexpected information.

"But it's *this weekend*," I finally spit out.

"I know."

This weekend, Saturday to be exact, is the five-year anniversary of our dad's death. It was lung cancer, it was an absolute nightmare, and now the actual day, April 16th, is completely cursed. Not only did my dad die on April 16th, but I've been broken up with on April 16th, I've gotten a flat tire on the freeway on April 16th, I had my school email account hacked on April 16th. It has been a five-year constant that my life, and Jordan's life, too, completely goes to shit on this day. The universe knows we're already suffering and decides to really dig that knife in and twist it around.

I lean back in my chair, out of the frame of the camera, and push my hands through my hair. "Do we really want to go somewhere? Shouldn't we just lock ourselves inside and ride it out with junk food and Netflix this time around instead of tempting fate?"

"I thought about that," Jordan says gently. "But then I also thought that Dad would have loved this festival. I mean, where else would he rather have been than surrounded by a bunch of bands? He lived for live music. This could be a way to, I don't know, kinda honor him. We'll be doing one of his favorite things, and we'll be together. There's no way we could have a bad day like that."

He does have a point here, and I rub my hands up and down my thighs as I mull it over. Jordan got his height from Dad, I inherited Dad's wavy blond hair, and he passed down his love of music to both of us. Dad, who was a radio DJ, wasn't exactly musical, and neither are we—I love to sing, but after a few unsuccessful auditions for children's theater and kids' choir, we all realized I was better suited to living room karaoke, while Jordan has at least three instruments stashed under his bed that he was never able to get past a month of lessons with. But both of us connect with music on a visceral level, even more so since Dad died. So, yeah, spending the anniversary of the day he died doing something we know he would have loved does seem like the perfect way to connect with him.

"And, you know, next year . . ." Jordan trails off, but he doesn't need to finish. The rest of his sentence has been appearing in my nightmares ever since he committed to Southern California University, our dream school and our parents' alma mater, to play basketball on a scholarship. I got into SCU, too, but I can only go if I get the huge scholarship I applied for, because we can't afford it otherwise. So, seeing my twin every day next year, like I have for the past eighteen years, and following in my parents' footsteps . . . well, it's all in the hands of a faceless scholarship committee. It's a committee headed up by my mom's boss, who specifically told me to apply, so I guess it's not completely faceless. But still.

There's a small chance that next year we may be separated.

There's a small chance that next year is going to suck.

He reaches across my desk and grabs my still-recording camera, turning it so it faces me. "So, Andi, do you want to go? To the best music festival in California? With the best brother in the world?"

I look directly into the lens. "We're going to Cabazon!" I scream.

Well, as soon as we get permission from Mom, anyway.

>>> • <<<

We find Mom sitting in the corner of our worn-in sectional couch, her laptop perched on her crossed legs. Spring has sprung in full force in Southern California, but my mom is still zipped up into her SCU hoodie like it's a cocoon, and I can guarantee her heated throw is turned up to at least medium. "I'm cold-blooded; I can't help it," Mom is fond of saying.

"Give me ten seconds," Mom says as we creep down the stairs. She doesn't even have to turn around to know that we have something we want to talk to her about. And as we get closer, I notice she's not working on her laptop like she's supposed to be. She's typing furiously on her phone and laughing gently while she shakes her head.

"I thought you were working," I say, coming up behind her and playfully pulling the hood off her head. Mom works from home managing all online and social media content for a group of local shopping centers. She has an office upstairs, but she often prefers the couch. "Easier access to the snacks," she says.

"I was, but then your grandma needed me to explain some memes she saw on Facebook. You know how confused she gets."

"Poor Grandma," Jordan says, leaning against the back of the couch. "Didn't she quit Facebook after she got in that fight with her neighbor?"

"She can never quit. Okay, done." Mom drops her phone onto a pillow. "Now, what's up, my children?" She pats the cushion next to her, motioning us to join her, but her aggressive patting sends the ever-present tall pile of envelopes at her side spilling all across the couch.

Since Dad's death, the envelopes have become his replacement in the house. The cancer tore us all wide open, but even worse than the trauma and unending grief of losing him is the flood of medical bills that never stop pouring through our door. His steadily growing ratings and status as LA's number two most popular morning DJ didn't matter when his station got bought out by some faceless, heartless megacompany and his entire morning show team got replaced like yesterday's cat litter. He lost his dream job, we lost our health insurance, and then, bam, cancer.

Oh, your father is dying in a horrible way? Here, let's have that awful death make you poor, too.

So, the tall pile of envelopes is like our own Leaning Tower of Pisa—impressively tall and headed for a fall any day now. But no one is taking cute pictures trying to prop this tower up; we're just crossing our fingers that there isn't a major collapse.

Before we can join Mom on the couch, she switches gears, pushing her laptop onto the envelope pile and hopping up. "Wait. I need to eat. Come with me."

We trail her into the kitchen, where she rummages through the pantry before giving up and opening the fridge.

"What do you need? A signature on something? A ride? An alibi?"

"We have a proposition for you," Jordan says.

"I'm listening." She grabs a tray of veggies from the fridge and slides it onto the dining table.

"This weekend is the Cabazon Valley Music and Arts Festival out in the desert—"

"Ah, yes. Your dad and I went to Cabazon one year."

"You did?" I'm not surprised; Mom and Dad had all kinds of fun pre-us, and even after, thanks to Dad's job. I'm more surprised that we've never heard her mention it. For a while, her Dad stories didn't get very far—the tears stopped them in their tracks. But lately it's been easier for her to talk about him. Just like it has for all of us, I guess.

"Yeah. It was the second or third year they had it, right before you kids were born." Mom's voice gets thick with nostalgia as she slides into one of the dining table chairs, taking on that misty, faraway tone she always gets when remembering her times spent with Dad. When she shifts into that voice, it's usually the signal of a good story coming. "Your dad got sent by the station. He got to interview Dave Grohl, who is, like, the nicest man alive. He bought us beers."

I want to hear more about Dave Grohl, but Jordan is a man on a mission. "Well, Sergio gave me two weekend passes he won because he can't go." He flops into the chair next to her and grabs a handful of baby carrots. "I don't think Foo Fighters are playing, but the Known are headlining."

"Oh, I love the Known! That Bernard White . . . mmm mmm mmm."

"Ew, Mom."

Mom smacks Jordan playfully on the arm. "What? I'm a human person. I'm allowed to find other human people attractive. When is it again?"

My brother and I exchange a quick look. "Uh, this weekend," I say. "We'd need to leave Thursday."

"I see." Mom slowly crunches on a bell pepper. "And I assume you would need to miss school on Friday. And Monday as well? And you'd be out there with no supervision—"

Jordan throws his hands up. "We're eighteen—"

"I just told you I have attended this festival, Jordan. I know exactly what kind of debauchery goes on there."

Just as I open my mouth to remind Mom what good, trustworthy children we are, my phone makes a noise. My email alert. From the email account I set up just for college stuff.

"Oh my God. It's my college email." I pull my phone out of my back pocket so quickly that it slips through my fingers and crashes onto the floor.

"Take a deep breath, sweetie," Mom says as she bends over to retrieve my phone.

"It's about the scholarship."

"Oh my God," Mom says, at the same time Jordan says, "Open it!"

My hand shakes as I try to focus on the notification. All the subject of the email says is *Geffen Achievement Scholarship*. Not even a hint to let me know what fate to prepare for. "I'm scared."

"Want me to do it?" Jordan grabs for my phone, but I snatch it away quickly.

"No, I've got it." One deep breath, and then I tap the notification, opening the email on my screen. A quick scan through the body of the email tells me exactly what I need to know.

Thank you . . .

However . . .

"I didn't get it." The words stick in my throat, and by the time they come out, I'm not even sure if Mom and Jordan can hear them. "I didn't get the scholarship."

"What? Why? You were supposed to be a shoo-in!"

The scholarship is sponsored by my mom's boss, Mr. Geffen. He owns this huge shopping center conglomerate, and he specifically told her that I should apply. That I was an ideal candidate and exactly the kind of student they wanted to give this money to. Mom said he actually winked at her when he passed along the information. He did everything but send out skywriting that I was going to get this money, and now his scanned signature is at the bottom of my rejection email.

"It doesn't say. Just thank you for applying, blah blah blah, many excellent candidates, blah blah blah, we wish you well, blah blah." I toss my phone onto the table, then rake my shaky fingers through my hair. "I didn't get the money."

We all look at one another, and we don't even need to say it. That pile of envelopes on the couch says it all.

We can't afford to pay for my tuition at SCU. And when I applied for this scholarship, Mom and I agreed that if I didn't get it, which we didn't think would be an issue, but just in case, I wouldn't take out loans for school. I've seen firsthand what debt can do. I don't want to end up with envelopes following me everywhere. I filled out the FAFSA, but when I saw I only qualified for loans, I rejected them all.

This scholarship was my only chance, and it's gone.

My parents met at SCU. It was their freshman year, and they had a class together—biology lab. Dad leaned over the lab table and asked Mom if she wanted to start a study group with him, and she said yes. For some reason, they each thought the other one was good at science, and they were both wrong. Their study group wasn't successful, but their partnership definitely was, and they were inseparable after that. Their relationship, everything about it, has always been a goal to me.

When I picture my life, my future, I always picture what my parents had. Walking through the quad at SCU.

Meeting my soul mate in a class. Majoring in communications like my dad. Cheering Jordan from the stands at the basketball arena.

Now what?

"Wait." Jordan's voice yanks me out of my crushed fantasy. "Remember what you said upstairs?"

"Um . . . that you owe me In-N-Out? I'm not really feeling it right now, Jordan."

"Not that. You said that all it takes is one video for YouTube to pick up and recommend, and your channel could go viral. Your channel, Andi. That's it. That's how you get the money."

I shake my head. "It's not that easy. You said it yourself. No video about BeDazzling a backpack is going to make enough money for SCU. I barely pay for gas with my YouTube ad revenue."

Silence settles between us because he knows I'm right. As much as my couple hundred subscribers and I really love crafting, it's not exactly a big draw for the masses.

But then Mom says, "What about Cabazon?"

"What do you mean?"

"It's been a while since your dad and I went, but I know this festival is still popular. I bet you could make a video at Cabazon that would get tons of views." She reaches over to place her hand over mine. "You're so creative, sweetie. You could come up with something really amazing."

"Wait," I say. "You're letting us go?"

Her mouth straightens into a line, and she sucks air in through her nose, like she's really thinking about something. Finally she says, "I'm letting you go if you agree to work your butt off while you're there finding a way to make a Cabazon video so spectacular that it gets promoted, gets tons of views, and helps you build a channel that can actually make you some money."

Mom wants me to go to SCU just as much as I want to—that's no secret. It's equally important to her, that vision of me walking the quad, meeting my soul mate in class. It was also important to Dad, whose dream was to become so influential in LA radio that he would get something—a fountain, a bench, a toilet, literally anything—named after him on campus. He used to talk to us about how proud he would be, wearing an SCU DAD sweatshirt to games, moving us into the same dorm building he used to live in. This school mattered so much to him. It matters so much to our family.

Filming a Cabazon video, a "lifestyle" video aimed just at getting views, would mean abandoning everything I've built with my little crafting channel. It goes against what I believe in as a content creator.

But SCU.

But Dad.

Dad.

"But you know what Saturday is."

Mom reaches up and pulls me down into a hug, her arms wrapped so tightly around me it takes my breath away for a quick second. I hug her back with the same force. Mom is a hugger, and she passed that down to me. "I know, sweetie. And I think he would really like this. He'll be there with you. You'll make him proud."

Thoughts of all the possibilities for the weekend tumble around my mind like a pile of clothes in the dryer. But ultimately it comes down to Dad.

"I'll do it," I say, pulling away just enough that I can rest my forehead against hers. "I have to try."

Mom smiles and pulls me back in tight. "That's my girl."

CHAPTER 2

>>> • <<<

TWENTY-FOUR HOURS LATER, MY FRIENDSHIP BRACELET
video has been abandoned like a busted-wheel shopping
cart in a parking lot, and Jordan and I have managed
to cobble together a collection of mismatched camping
gear for our adventure. We also scoured the Cabazon
Valley music festival message boards to make a list of the
food and supplies we'll need to survive the weekend. Our
preparation is haphazard at best, and I'm convinced we're
missing at least ten critical items and have packed about
five things we absolutely don't need, including an emergency coloring book and a fancy dress, but Jordan insists
that sloppy, negligent packing is all part of the experience. And since he's an entire five-and-a-half minutes
older and constantly reminds me of this fact, I usually go
ahead and defer to his infinite wisdom.

We climb into our shared Toyota Highlander, our
dad's old car, and drive it through stop-and-go LA traffic
and then the wide-open California desert. Jordan drives,

Google Maps navigates, and I spend my time glued to my phone researching potential angles for this game-changing video I have promised Mom.

"Look," I say, pointing my phone screen toward him, "there's this band called Damnation Dalmatian. Their fans all wear black and white polka dots to their shows. Maybe there are some other bands that inspire weird fashion choices and I can make a video about that."

"See my hands on this big wheel here?" he says playfully. "That means I'm driving. I can't exactly look right now."

Undeterred, I pull my phone back and continue scrolling. "Oooh, maybe I can find people who made their own festival clothes. I can interview them like Dad used to for the station." My dad was known for his funny interviews of people on the street. He had this collection of random questions, and he somehow always managed to get the most incredible answers out of people.

"But . . ." I chew on my bottom lip as I scan the photos of previous years' festivalgoers in their runway-ready looks. "What if I do make a fashion video, and it takes off? Will all these new subscribers expect fashion content? Do I know enough about fashion to churn out regular videos about clothes and stuff?" One glance down at my Old Navy tank top and shorts answers that question for me. Sure, I hand-embroidered tiny daisies along the pockets of these shorts, but that's nothing compared to the influencers out there who look straight out of Fashion Week.

"Fashion isn't so far off from crafting," he says with a shrug, as if we really do have some kind of twin mind reading. "Maybe they make their own polka-dot shirts."

"But completely changing what I do for one weekend isn't going to do anything for me. I've spent time building a brand."

Jordan sneaks a glance at me. "Yeah, but does anyone care about that brand?"

"Ouch, dude." I reach across the center console and smack him hard on the arm. "I care about it. That's what matters. I don't get on you for being all about basketball. Why are you crapping all over my stuff?"

"You know I love your stuff. That's not what I mean. I'm just saying that making friendship bracelets in the middle of the desert isn't going to get you followers, so focus on what will and figure out how you can fit into it."

"So, I fit into it and then what?" I snap. "Completely switch over to fashion videos forever after I get all these subscribers? Or do I bait and switch and go back to making my own wrapping paper, and they'll all unsubscribe? How is that going to pay for SCU?"

Jordan gives me another shrug and a small smile, and I slump down into my seat. This is going to be impossible. I got so caught up in the idea that I gave no thought to the reality of how hard it is to come up with good video content.

I spend another hour exploring the depths of the internet for ideas, Jordan's words still aggravating me like a bug bite I can't stop scratching, pushing me to search weirder and more random topics. But when I get to a *BuzzFeed* list about Cabazon porta-potty etiquette, I recognize it's time for a break, so in an effort to clear my mind, I drop my phone into my lap and stare mindlessly out at the expanse of dirt, sparse grass, and tall windmills that pepper the desert landscape zooming along outside the window.

But, as usual, when I have a clear mind, my thoughts turn to Dad.

"Do you think this is a good idea?" I finally say.

My words come out so quietly, I'm not sure Jordan hears me. But after a pause, he turns down the volume on his playlist and peeks at me from the corner of his eye. "Well, we're almost there, so it better be."

"I mean, running away here instead of staying home and being sad."

Jordan sighs. "I've been thinking about that. But I keep going back to what Mom said. Dad would love this. He would want us to be here."

I draw my legs up onto the seat and wrap my arms around them, pulling myself as close as I can manage with a seat belt in the way. "I just don't know the right way to feel."

"I don't think there is a right way." He reaches over to give a comforting pat to my knee. "You just feel what you feel."

"I know, but at first I was sad all the time, and I know that was normal. But now it's been five years, and I don't know how this is supposed to go. I'm not sad all the time now, but when I am, it's this all-encompassing sadness that doesn't leave room for anything else. And when I catch myself not feeling sad, I feel awful about that. Like, how dare I be happy when my dad is dead? Do you feel like that, too?"

"That's exactly how I feel. All the time."

It's comforting to hear that Jordan struggles with the same feelings that I do, and I relax, stretching my legs back out in front of me and leaning my head on the headrest. One of Mom's cousins died in a car accident when they were kids, and Mom always says that when she sees a butterfly, she knows it's her cousin Lucy saying hi, letting Mom know she's still around.

My dad loved music. It was his job and his passion and his entire life. Maybe music is like his butterfly. Something special between us. His way of letting me know he's here.

Maybe he will be here at this festival with us this weekend.

"I just miss him," I say, turning to face the windmills and the desert.

"I do, too," Jordan says. He turns the volume back up on his playlist right as a new song starts. It's Foo Fighters. Dave Grohl.

Dad's here.

>>> • <<<

When we pull off the freeway in Palm Desert, almost three hours after we left the house, thanks to traffic, the mid-April California heat is oppressive, even with the sun beginning to set, and I'm no closer to having a video topic than I was when we left.

We follow the endless line of cars to the huge polo fields that hold the festival each year, and, finally, after an hour of waiting, getting searched, and being directed here and there, we pull into our car camping spot—a small chalked-off space for the Highlander and a small chalked-off space for us to set up our tent. Our home, dirty home for the weekend.

It takes about five minutes for us to pull everything out of the back of the Highlander and about five minutes and fifteen seconds to realize that, Houston, we have a major problem.

"It's dark," Jordan says, scratching the back of his closely shaved head as he stares down at our hodgepodge pile of camping supplies. The field of campsites we're parked on is divided up into streets with names and street signs, like a cute little neighborhood, and it seems everyone on East 118th Street jumped into immediate action. Tents, E-Z Ups, and other structures pop up and down our row of campsites, with people scrambling around loudly and furiously to get their temporary homes built.

"Is there a flashlight or something in there?" I frown down at our pile, in disbelief that between the two of us, both honors students who got into SCU, neither one of us considered, hey, maybe we need some kind of light source for sleeping in the middle of the desert for three nights.

He shrugs. "I don't believe there is."

"Of course not. Why would there be?" It's one of those situations where I have to laugh because it's all so ridiculous. "And even if we could see, would you have any idea how to assemble this tent?"

He shrugs again and laughs. "Mr. Nguyen said it was a no-brainer when he let me borrow it."

I roll my eyes like it's no big deal, but my neck and shoulders pull tight with tension and my blood pumps faster through my veins. We assembled this pile of supplies together, but he promised me he had all the camping stuff under control, like borrowing this tent from our neighbor across the street. My brother always assures me he has the details handled, and he never, ever does. And the worst part is that he does this every single time, so it's not even a surprise. This is just as much my fault for trusting him. I swear, this is why I need to make sure I get myself to SCU next year. There's no way Jordan can function without me.

"We have the flashlights on our phones," I suggest. "Or we can turn the car headlights on. But we'll have to do it fast. We don't want to drain the batteries."

"I guess," he says. We both stare helplessly down at the pile of tent and tarp and camping stuff on the ground in front of us, and we stay like that for a good minute before Jordan's phone pings with a text.

"No way," he says, looking down to his phone.

"Is that God?" I ask. "Is he saying let there be light?"

"Even better." Jordan laughs and shoves his phone into his back pocket. "It's Monica Martinez."

"Who?"

"You know that hot volleyball player from school? With the hair? Her brother is in all the plays? She posted yesterday that she'd be here this weekend, and I told her we would, too, and I told her to text me. And she totally did."

My eyebrows shoot up to my hairline. "And how does this make her better than God?"

"Because she's on East 107th Street setting up camp right this minute, and I bet you a million Baconators she didn't forget a freaking flashlight."

"So you're going to leave me here? With this?" I kick the pile of tentpoles on the ground in front of us, and I remember too late that I'm wearing flip-flops.

My brother doesn't even notice that I'm hobbling around in pain. He's already halfway to Monica Martinez's campsite. "It will just be a minute. I promise," he says, waving as he walks off. "See if you can get something done without me!"

There's no doubt that it's going to be at least an hour before he gets back, if he comes back at all. Even when he has the best of intentions, Jordan is so easily derailed by shiny objects it's a little embarrassing. I mean, I'm sure he didn't plan to ditch me at the first sight of a hot girl. Or maybe he did, and he didn't think the first sight would come this quickly. Either way, I'm going to be alone in the dark for a while now, so I better see what I can do here with my brains and my cell phone light. With this free time, I'd totally sit down and record a bit for the video if I actually had some decent lighting. Or an idea. My battery-powered ring light is in my duffel, so I guess it's time to go digging for it, and then set up to film . . . something. Film myself setting up? Multitasking at its best.

"Need some help?"

For some reason, the guy's voice behind me sounds super familiar, and for a hot second, I run through my mental contacts list trying to place it.

But as I turn around, I see the guy standing next to the Highlander is clearly not someone I know. He has brown skin and black hair . . . maybe Indian? It's tough to tell in this bad light. He has an LA Dodgers baseball hat on, pulled down low on his head, and he's wearing a tank top, board shorts, and flip-flops—the unofficial uniform for guys at Cabazon, according to the message boards and photo feeds Jordan and I scoured before we left.

And he is really freaking hot.

I must be staring at him without speaking for longer than is socially appropriate, because he backs up a few steps and puts his hands up in a surrender. "Sorry. Didn't mean to bother you."

"Wait," I say. "Sorry, you just surprised me." I wave at the pile of poles and nylon at my feet. "So, did a Helpless Girl alarm go off and send you to the rescue?"

The guy smiles, and I'm glad he does, because even in the dark I can tell he has a full, gorgeous smile and perfect teeth. I'm a sucker for a guy with perfect teeth. "Being a girl has nothing do with it. And I don't think you look helpless, I think you look like a person trying to figure out how to assemble a tent alone in the dark. I'm pretty sure anyone would struggle with that task." He takes a few steps closer and scans my dark campsite. "Don't you have a flashlight or anything?"

I let out a laugh. "Nope. My brother went to track

one down, but, honestly, I think I may have lost him for the night."

"Well, I have a lantern over at my tent." He points to the camp space directly across the makeshift street from ours, where a large tent and an E-Z Up are already set up between two shiny trucks. His two-space campsite already resembles a four-star resort. "Why don't I go get it, and then I can help you out?"

"Wow. Yeah. That would be cool." I mutter a thank-you in his direction, but he's already trotting across the way to his campsite to grab the lantern.

He's back within the minute, bent over the pile of supplies and helping me assemble the small tent Jordan and I will share, which is shockingly easier when I can actually kinda see. Everything is still cloaked in shadows, thanks to the short reach of the guy's lantern, but working with him on this task is quick and pleasant. He doesn't bark out orders like my dad used to, he doesn't make me do all the work and claim to be supervising like Mom always does, and he doesn't leave me all the useless tasks because I'm little, which is Jordan's usual attitude. With the guy's help, the whole thing is put together in under fifteen minutes.

"Perfection," he says as he steps on the last of the tent stakes to drive it into the soft dirt of the campsite. "Your brother should be pretty impressed when he comes back and sees this."

"Thank you so much. I owe you big-time." I shake my head as I wipe my hands down the back of my shorts. "I still can't believe we brought a camp stove and enough bacon to last for two weeks, and we didn't think to bring a flashlight. Amateur hour over here."

He laughs, showing off those perfect teeth again. "Well, you can pay me back by sharing some of that bacon tomorrow, and we'll call it even." He sticks out his hand. "What's your name?"

"I'm Andi." I stare at his offered hand, and as I reach out to shake it, my body reacts without running it by my brain at all, and I pull him all the way in for a quick hug. As soon as I do it, I'm flooded with stranger danger plus the mortification of having thrown myself at a dude I just met, and it all morphs into this sudden need to push him away as quickly as I pulled him in.

As I do, I notice a few things about him, aside from the genuine look of surprise on his face. One, during the few seconds of that hug, I fit perfectly into his chest, like a puzzle piece. Two, his tank top smells like the same detergent we use at home, and I'm pleased to notice it doesn't smell like cigarettes. There is nothing more of a deal breaker than a guy who smokes, and it seems I always meet smokers at concerts. And, three, his biceps. He has glorious, glorious biceps that, somehow, I missed when he first walked up and even when he was helping me put the tent together. Damn bad lighting.

But God, Andi, he's a strange guy in the dark. Get yourself together.

"So, was that a hug, or . . . ?" he says, but he's laughing. And he's looking at me in this way that lets me know he's totally fine with whatever it was. "Where are you from, Andi?"

"LA." Desperate for something to do so we can move on from that hug, I unfold the two camping chairs Jordan and I found in a dusty corner of our garage and set them up for us in front of the newly assembled tent. There's something about this festival atmosphere; it's already worlds away from my real, normal life at home, and it has clearly already soaked into me. Last night I would have never imagined myself inviting some complete stranger, no matter how hot, to hang out with me in the dark. But tonight? There are no strangers at Cabazon. And just because I embarrassed myself doesn't mean I'm ready for him to leave. "You?"

"Nice." He stretches out in the chair, crossing his long legs at the ankles and lacing his fingers behind his head. "I'm from South Bay. Redondo Beach. I'm here with my older brother."

"Oh, me, too. Well, he's my twin brother, actually, but technically he's older. And we live in Pasadena." I explain how Jordan's friend gave him the festival tickets and we came here last minute. I leave out all the parts about filming a video, trying to figure out how I can get myself to college, and my dad's looming deathaversary. Talk about too much information.

"Well, that certainly explains your lack of lantern." He stands up and stretches, and I can't help but notice that when he reaches his arms up, his tank top lifts and exposes the small strip of skin above his board shorts. Are there abs under there? Is this guy for real?

I'm afraid him standing up means he's going to leave, but I want this night to keep stretching on like that shirt of his. This campsite and the dark and the stars make tonight feel almost otherworldly, separated from reality in the most surreal and exciting way.

"So, which bands are you here to see?" The Cabazon Valley Music and Arts Festival is host to over one hundred bands and artists on five different stages throughout the course of the weekend, so there's a chance we could go through the whole thing and never once see the same band. Or each other.

But those fears are squashed when he pulls out a list he made of all the bands he's hoping to catch, and I spot several of the bands I have starred in the festival app.

I point to a local Pasadena band. "You like the Gold Parade?"

"Oh, yeah," he says, his face lighting up. "They're one of my favorites. You ever see them play?"

Next to crafting, talking music is my favorite, so once he gets me going, I yak his ear off about the time I saw the

Gold Parade play at a warehouse party with only thirty people in the crowd, and he comes back at me with the time he saw Tarot Card, another LA band on the lineup this weekend, play a surprise show at an all-ages club in Hollywood.

We talk music until we're interrupted by his text. "Ugh. I should probably go back to my brother," he says, jerking his head toward his campsite across the way. "He's missing this lantern and being a real dick to me about it."

"Oh, sorry." I stick my hands in the front pockets of my shorts, then I pull them out and stick them in the back pockets instead. "I don't want to cause family drama."

He shakes his head. "No worries. But, um. We should totally meet up for the Gold Parade tomorrow. I mean, if you want to."

An army of butterflies takes flight in my stomach. Is this hot guy seriously asking me to hang out? Is he going to hand me a blank check next?

"Well." I try to keep my voice steady, even though I really want to scream or laugh or something at how awesome this night has turned since Jordan walked off. "I am going to check them out for sure. And if you're going, too . . ."

"Looking forward to it, then," he says, giving me this huge smile that makes me want to float away like a hot-air balloon over the desert.

"Oh, wait. Before you go." I pull my phone out of my back pocket. "I'm doing this thing where I'm documenting my weekend. First time at Cabazon and all."

"I get it. You want me to take a picture of you and your tent?"

"No, silly. I need a picture with you. But we can try to get the tent in the background." Again, I wish my ring light wasn't buried in my bag, but I don't want to push my luck by asking him to wait while I dig around in my duffel so this shot is well-lit. My lighting needs are hard to explain to outsiders, so the flash will have to do.

I scoot myself so I'm right up against him, my back making contact with his chest. I stretch my T. rex arm out for a selfie.

"I'll get it," he says, and he gently grabs the phone from my hand, brushing my fingers as he takes it from me. His arm is long and his glorious bicep is right by my ear, and somewhere in the back of my mind, I think about telling him that I have a mini tripod in the back of the car, but I somehow lose my head a little while I'm pressed up against him, and he snaps the picture.

"Check it out," he says as he hands my phone back to me, but I can't even manage to look. I'm too caught up in the buzz his biceps left on my ear and the sting of the flash in my eyes. "Is it good?"

"What? Oh, yeah, it's great." I shove my phone in my

pocket and shift around. Jeez, Andi. Make words come out of your mouth.

He doesn't leave like I thought he would. He's still standing there, and he's looking at me, smiling and expectant, so I look back. We stand there and stare at each other, both of us grinning like goofs, for what feels like ten minutes but is probably more like fifteen seconds. However long it is, it's past the length that two people who just met should be gaping at each other. There's that Cabazon festival magic again, making this charged moment between us feel like it's crackling with electricity and exploding with promise instead of awkward as hell.

"It was awesome meeting you," he says finally. "But I really do have to go. I'll pop back over tomorrow morning." He picks up his lantern and trots off, disappearing behind the sheet hanging down the front of his E-Z Up, like a desert mirage.

"What just happened?" I ask myself out loud as I crawl into my tent. It occurs to me as I change into my pajamas that I gave him my name, but I never got his. Is that another normal festival thing? Should I have not given him my name or made up some alias? I'll have to ask Jordan about that in the morning.

The whole drive here, I stared out the window and watched the desert zoom by, wondering if there was any hope for me this weekend. How would this all work out if I had no good ideas, no definite plan? I had no hope that I'd actually find a way to end up at SCU next year like I want to be.

On the way here, I felt like maybe this weekend was a mistake.

But now, it feels like a turning point. Like maybe something will work out for me after all.

CHAPTER 3

>>> • <<<

FRIDAY MORNING, JORDAN SHUFFLES UP TO ME WHERE
I'm waiting in the never-ending line for the campground
shower facility, his towel around his neck and his manly
all-in-one shampoo/conditioner/body wash in his hand.
How do guys get away with one single product for all
their parts while I have an entire basket in my arms?
Although it's really going to take more than a squirt of
that product to wash away the dead-behind-the-eyes look
on his face and the imprint of the pillow that seems to be
carved into his cheek.

He fumbled his way back into our tent about one
hour before the obnoxious dudebros at the campsite next
to us finally turned down—but not off—the awful white
boy reggae music they blasted at full volume all night
long. That was only about an hour and a half before I got
up for early morning festival yoga, so I'd guess Jordan's
running on about two hours of sleep right about now.

"Yo," he mumbles.

"How did that flashlight retrieval operation go last night?" Yoga gave me a little zen, but the fact that my annoyance at my brother creeps into my voice immediately is beyond my control.

"You got the tent up just fine."

"Yeah, because someone from the campsite across the way came over with a big lantern and helped me."

"Whatever," he mutters, running his hand back and forth over his shaved head.

"Was it worthwhile, at least? Ditching me in the dark and leaving me to fend for myself?"

"I don't want to talk about it."

I love my brother, obviously. We were in the womb together. He's been my best friend since the second we were born. But we couldn't be more different. I'm super driven, organized, and type A, while my brother is sweet and charming and a bit of a mess. He follows his gut and his heart, wherever they lead, and he doesn't think about the consequences. Jordan didn't maliciously plan to leave me alone in the dark to assemble the tent on my own. And I could bring up the various scenarios that could have taken place last night, such as getting abducted, drugged, murdered, etc., and he would feel terrible for the rest of the day. But that wouldn't change the future. He'd still do it again tonight. For another hot girl. For a game of pickup basketball. For free food.

I always say I don't give second chances; it was my

dad's motto—he said people will always let you down, and he was kinda proven right after his station laid him off. But Jordan is my twin brother, so it's not like I can *not* give him second, or third, or seventy-fifth chances. Dad was right, though. Jordan always, always, always does something that lets me down. I guess that's why I feel like I need to keep an eye on him all the time. If he's like this with me watching out for him, what kind of mess will he be all on his own?

We discuss our plans for the day, and I try to keep it casual when I mention the guy from across the way and the fact that we made a plan to meet up for the Gold Parade.

"Oooh, you can't even be mad at me for ditching you for a hot girl when you already found yourself a dude."

"What? No! It's not like that." Apparently, it didn't come out as casual as I'd hoped. "I'm just saying the guy who helped me with the tent liked a lot of the same bands as me, and we're going to hang out. He was cool. That's all. Stop putting words in my mouth."

"Look at you! You're turning as red as your towel. You're such a bad liar."

"To quote you, I don't want to talk about it."

"Fair enough."

It's finally our turn to shower, and the whole ordeal is neither comfortable nor fun. From the outside, the shower structure looks like one of those portable classrooms on the outskirts of our school's campus, and inside is nothing but showerheads on the walls and drains clogged with multicolored hairballs on the floor and about twenty people in bathing suits and shower shoes trying to get as clean as possible as quickly as possible. It's awkward and inefficient—showering in a bikini has never really been all that effective—but at least I don't feel like I'm covered in a layer of sweaty dust when I'm done.

We flip-flop back to our campsite, put our stuff away, change, and get started on our epic breakfast. I'm going to need energy to get going on this video.

"We should probably text Mom," Jordan says. "Let her know we're up and at 'em and making a nutritious meal." Mom helped us grocery shop for our food supplies, and she packed up the fixings for some awesome breakfast burritos. "You do that, and I'll pour you some cold brew."

I grab my phone off the portable charger, where I left it while I went to early morning festival yoga and the shower. Mom is probably sitting on top of her phone waiting to hear from us, and she is for sure going to ask about my video, but I'd rather not talk to her about it until I have everything all figured out. Or at least something figured out, anyway. The last thing I want is to hear her disappointed voice so soon into the weekend.

To stall a bit, I sip the cold brew and poke absently at apps on my phone as I plan out how to steer Mom away from asking about all things video without being too obvious about it. I open up my camera roll, bringing the photo of me and the guy from last night to full size on my screen.

And that's when my world comes crashing down around me.

The guy. I recognize him.

The guy from across the way is Jay Bankar.

I know Jay Bankar. And I absolutely hate him.

My stomach bottoms out, and I lower myself to the ground.

"Jay Bankar," I mumble.

"What?" Jordan is starting the cooking on our camp stove, but he turns around to see what I'm doing. "Why are you flopped on the floor? Get up."

"Jay Bankar," I say, louder this time.

"Ew. What about him? Is he here?" Jordan has heard so many of my Jay Bankar rants he can practically recite them himself.

"Jay Bankar is the guy."

"What guy?"

"The tent guy. The guy from last night."

Before I have a chance to process any of this, a head pokes around the opening of our campsite.

"Does last night's bacon offer still stand?"

And now, in the light of day, with a clear head, it's so, so obvious. I've seen that face, the smooth, brown skin, the wide, white smile, the messy black hair so many times online, I'm shocked I didn't recognize it immediately. And his voice. His voice practically triggers my vomit reflex when I hear it through my phone speaker. I can't believe I had such a long conversation with him without barfing.

He was just so unexpected. I mean, aside from the fact that it was pretty dark, he was completely out of context, like seeing your math teacher at a house party or something. But even more than that, it was because he was actually nice. Jay Bankar is many things, but nice has never, ever been one of them. The guy is a walking, talking, flaming turd.

Oh my God, Jay Bankar is here and just asked me a question, and I am on the ground freaking out. Must get up. Must get rid of him. "Oh, sorry. We don't have any more bacon." My voice is icy cold, and I don't even feel bad when I see his smile fall.

"Oh," he says. "That's fine, I was just—"

"Thanks again for the tent and all, but . . ." I shrug. I don't have a plan for finishing that sentence, but I want Jay Bankar off my campsite immediately. "My brother is back now, so you don't have to check up on me or anything. You can go, actually."

Jay Bankar's face twists up in confusion. "Oh. I thought . . ." He looks from me, who has let my long hair fall across the side of my face like a curtain, blocking all access, to Jordan, who is aggressively avoiding eye contact by putting all his focus on the Egg Beaters he's pouring into our little skillet. "I guess I was wrong. Have a good day. Maybe I'll see you around." He shoves his hands into the pockets of his shorts and turns toward his campsite.

"Probably not," I say to his back.

"Damn, girl," Jordan says. "Where did that come from? I've never heard you be so bitchy before in my life."

He's right. I'm not that bitchy, ever. I even won "Most Likely to Help a Chicken Cross the Road" in eighth grade. But this is Jay Bankar. He tricked me into thinking he was a decent person, and now he wants to eat my bacon. Nope nope nope.

"Let me know when breakfast is done," I say to Jordan, slamming the door on any further discussion of this topic. Instead I slide through the opening of our tent as quickly as possible so Jay doesn't catch a glimpse of me, and I flop down on my air mattress, where I stare at the picture of us from the night before on my phone.

Yup, now that I look at it, the guy I was snuggled up to in this photo is most definitely Jay Bankar, revolting YouTube personality. Jay Bankar, who plays pranks on people and films them for his channel so he and his hordes of followers can ridicule them in the comment section. Jay Bankar, who has smashed people's phones, stolen people's dogs, and pushed people into a small lake, all in the name of raking up subscriptions, views, and ad revenue. Jay Bankar, who even faked getting hit by a car to prank his own sweet Indian grandma and then posted it on YouTube for likes. That particular pile of crap is one of his most popular videos.

Jay Bankar is quite literally the grossest human being ever, and I've always sworn if I ever saw him in person, I would make sure he knew what I thought about him. But here I was, taking pictures of us snuggling.

My heart sinks remembering the hope that filled me up as I drifted off to sleep last night. How often does it happen that you meet a guy, a hot guy at that, and just immediately click? And you can tell he feels the same way? It's never happened to me, that's for sure, and I'd never even considered that it could. My body buzzed with the excitement, the promise of it all night long.

And now it's all for nothing, gone in a puff of smoke.

Thank God I didn't post that photo of the two of us. I'd never be able to show my face online again. No one would ever believe that I just didn't recognize a fellow YouTuber who has hundreds of thousands of subscribers. Or that Jay Bankar, who is awful and rude and once said that anyone stupid enough to fall for one of his pranks deserved what they got, is actually the sweet, charming guy I met last night. The guy who helped me with my tent and liked the same music and laughed at my jokes and genuinely seemed to want to hang out with me some more.

I shouldn't be so attached already, but, damn. I guess that version of him is all an act. Nothing that happened between us was real, and I let it all out with a sigh of disappointment.

My phone vibrates with a call from Mom, snapping me out of my bummed-out thoughts about Jay Bankar, America's Worst Human. She must have been able to sense my distress with her mom radar.

"I'm surprised I haven't heard from you yet," she says when I answer the phone.

I let out another long sigh as I sit up. "I was just about to call you, actually. But I got distracted by a wandering asshole."

"Well, that sounds alarming. Is everything okay?"

"Fine. Dandy. Couldn't be better." Mom is always a good choice for talking through my issues, but this . . . whatever just happened with Jay is too fresh. I can't help but feel ridiculous over this stab of betrayal from a practical stranger, and Mom will probably give me crap about wasting time flirting instead of getting down to business on my video. "Got the campsite set up no problem last night. Jordan's making breakfast, and we're heading into the festival after we eat. Absolutely not about to have a meltdown. It's all sunshine and roses over here."

Mom laughs. "I get the sense that you don't want to talk about it, but please promise to tell me if you are in any kind of actual trouble."

"Promise."

"And are things going as smoothly with your sure-to-be-amazing video?"

"You know it."

"What angle did you decide on?"

"Well, uh, Jordan and I have it narrowed down to a few pretty great ideas. We're going to explore the options once we get into the festival." Blowing Mom off like this, when my video is the reason she agreed to let us come here in the first place, makes me feel gross. I need to end this phone call immediately. "Want to talk to him? I'll get him right now. Love you." And before she has a chance to reply, I crawl out of the tent and hand my phone off to my brother.

Positioning my folding chair so my back is to Jay Bankar's campsite, I settle in with the breakfast burrito and fruit that Jordan had ready for me. His conversation with Mom is about as quick as mine was and full of promises to update her more when we have our "vision for the video that will change Andi's future" planned out.

"You okay?" Jordan asks as he tosses my phone back to me.

"No," I say through a mouthful of breakfast burrito, which is every bit as delicious as I hoped it would be.

"So, what happened last night?"

"Oh, now he wants to know."

"I made you breakfast," he says as he pulls his folding chair up across from mine. "You give me a story."

I fill my brother in on the events of the previous night as we both polish off our food.

"And you didn't recognize him at all?" Jordan's eyes wander to a group of white girls in bikinis walking by on their way to the shower. He waves at them, and I smack him on the knee.

"No! He was totally out of context. Why would I know the random person helping me with my tent in the middle of the desert? And it was dark because someone never came back with a flashlight—"

"You said he had a lantern!"

"And he had a hat on. And he was out of context!"

"You said that already."

Our tent neighbors decide it's a good time to turn the volume on their dance party back up again, this time with some EDM. I let out a long sigh, both at my Jay Bankar story and the onslaught of Hardwell. "If he was an asshole like he normally is, I would have known for sure."

"Well, now you know." Jordan leans over and pats my knee. "It's a good thing you didn't actually hang out with him. You probably would've been the star of his next prank video."

"Oh my God, you're right. I bet that's why he was nice! He was trying to get me to hang out with him so he could prank me and make fun of me for a video." I cover my face with my hands. "I can't believe I almost fell for it."

"Well, let's take this rage and put it to use. You have your own video to film this weekend so you can go to college with me. And we have bands to see and plans to make and fun to have. Gates open at noon, and I want to do as much as possible."

I shake off Jay Bankar's bad vibes and pull the festival schedule and map, both of which I've highlighted and annotated in my cutest hand-lettering, from my back pocket. There is an app, of course, but it's Day One, and I'm already all about battery conservation.

There are five stages at the Cabazon Valley Music and Arts Festival. The Main Stage and the Outdoor Stage—which is a stupid name because all the stages are outdoors—are the biggest, and the other three smaller stages are all named after something desert-y. Aside from some slight overlap between the Cactus Stage and the Outdoor Stage early in the evening, it appears we've lucked out on set times, and we still have plenty of gaps here and there for filming . . . just as soon as we decide on what it is we are going to film.

As long as I can avoid Jay Bankar for the rest of this festival and come up with and execute a life-changing video idea, everything will be just fine.

⟩⟩⟩ • ⟨⟨⟨

Row after neatly arranged row of car campsites branch out from one another on little streets like ours, and festivalgoers of all shapes and sizes wander between them.

Some play loud music, some sit on lawn chairs in front of their tents drinking beers, some have dance parties in the middle of the grassy streets. Everyone seems to be set up and happy, and the energy pulsing from the campground invigorates me. I feel like skipping down the walkway, I'm so amped up, and I can't help but imagine my mom and dad here in their younger days, walking this same walkway. Dad started us so young, taking us along to the concerts he worked for his radio station when we were barely out of diapers, and I know he must have felt so at home here in this diverse crowd. Music people were his kind of people, and walking this path feels like we're literally walking in his footsteps.

The crowd diversifies even more as we approach the main festival entrance, and I pull my vlog camera out of the belt bag I BeDazzled, getting great shots of all of the crowds of festivalgoers dancing, singing, and holding on to one another to use for B-roll. No matter what I end up focusing on in this video, I'll be able to use this footage somewhere.

Here at the entrance we merge with the drive-in crowd. These are the people staying in hotels and fancy rental homes in Palm Springs, who dress like this empty field in the middle of the desert is some kind of fashion runway. There are also a ton of celebrities at this festival every year, but I assume they have their own special entrance. It would be awesome to get some pics or video of someone famous, though. I'll have to keep my eyes peeled.

There's a line of both campers and drivers, so we merge into it, really joining this crowd for the first time instead of just watching it from behind my camera. With each shuffle forward, my excitement builds, to the point that by the time it's our turn, I'm clutching Jordan's arm hard enough that he swats me away. Finally, Jordan's backpack and my belt bag are checked, our wristbands are scanned, and we're in. It's festival time!

"Andi, look." The second we walk in, Jordan grabs my arm and pulls me to a stop. We're surrounded by so many things—booths, stands, strange artwork poking out of the grass—that at first I have no idea what I'm supposed to be looking at. The girl wearing pasties as a top? The guy in a kilt? The group in front of us in matching WILL DANCE FOR MOLLY T-shirts?

But one quick scan of the perimeter, and I figure it out. It's a pop-up tent with the Mobilocity logo emblazoned on it. And in front of the tent is a chalkboard sign sloppily hand-lettered with SOCIAL MEDIA INFLUENCERS CHECK IN HERE FOR VIP EXPERIENCE!

"I wonder what you get," Jordan says, elbowing me. "Maybe they let you go backstage or something."

"That's probably for established influencers." I love my little fan base. They've grown slowly, but they're dedicated and passionate, and their comments on my videos make my day. I'd be a damn liar, though, if I said there were a lot of them. And the only influencing I've done was when a family-owned yarn company sent me a few free skeins in exchange for posting about them on one of my crocheting features. I'd been pretty proud of that little sponsorship deal until right this second, when met with the idea of walking into this booth and calling myself a social media influencer with a straight face. "Mobilocity isn't exactly Samsung, anyway. I doubt they have that kind of access."

"Well, it's worth a look, right?" Jordan asks.

"I don't know. I doubt—"

"Andi, stop it. Stuff like this is how you grow your channel. How you make money off of it. How you get to SCU. Stop acting like you're not good enough."

"Fine. You're right." I take a deep breath and check the time on my phone. "The first band we want to see doesn't go on for about an hour and a half, and we had this time slotted for video prep anyway. Let's do this."

As we approach the tent, we're greeted by a hipster-looking white guy in what appears to be a vintage T-shirt but, upon closer inspection, is actually a Mobilocity T-shirt designed to look vintage. Hmm. I wonder if that's a real beard or just a clip-on.

"Hey." He leans against a card table in the tent in a way that's supposed to be casual, but its overcasualness makes it seem even more preplanned than it probably is. He drums his fingers on the table to the beat of the music playing from a Bluetooth speaker on the table. "I'm Matthew. How are you folks today? Stoked to be at Cabazon?" He smiles a too-big smile through his perfectly manicured beard. I wonder how long it took to grow that thing, and I wonder if it is part of his contract with Mobilocity. *Under no circumstances will I shave my hipster beard, upon penalty of relocation to the mail room.*

"Hey, Matthew." Jordan pulls out the fake hey-bro voice he uses with guys he's meeting for the first time. "We're super stoked. What about you?"

"Oh, yeah." Matthew leans some more. "Stoked beyond belief. What's your name?" He straightens up and offers his hand to my brother.

Jordan shakes his hand, and I wait for Matthew to turn to me and offer his hand or ask for my name, but he doesn't.

"So, I take it you saw our sign out there? We have a killer opportunity for social media influencers that's going to be super fun, give you unprecedented access to the festival, and get you a chance to go backstage and score an exclusive interview with the Known before they headline the show on Sunday. You interested?"

Jordan snorts, and I roll my eyes. This happens to us so often. No one ever confuses me for the county champion point guard or assumes that my help is the only reason Jordan is passing his honors classes. But if people hear that one of those Kennedy twins has a YouTube channel, everyone always jumps to him. Like he got the Y chromosome and all the height, so he must have gotten all the creativity and talent, too. I got left with the hair and the boobs, I guess.

Sure, I could have corrected Hipster Matthew right off the bat, but instead we let him talk just long enough that he'll be embarrassed when we tell him the real deal. Finally, Jordan interrupts him.

"Actually, my sister is the social media influencer." Jordan manages to say it with air quotes even without moving his fingers. "I just ride her coattails."

Hipster Matthew turns a few shades of red under his carefully cultivated beard. "No way!" he says. "What do you do online?"

I suck in a deep breath and picture myself on SCU's campus next year before I pull my shoulders back and answer him. "Oh, I have a YouTube channel. It's all about crafting and craft projects with a super targeted and enthusiastic audience. But I'm here this weekend because I'm thinking of branching out. Scoping out ideas for possible music-focused videos and networking." I peek at Jordan from the corner of my eye to see if I pulled off the confident businesswoman vibe I was going for, and he gives a small nod.

It must have worked, because Hipster Matthew clearly

has no idea what to make of me. Not only did he not think I came in here with anything to offer, he didn't seem to expect me to have anything of value to share. Honestly, I didn't feel like much of an influencer when I walked into this dumb Mobilocity booth, but the second he seemed to doubt me was the second I stopped doubting myself.

He lets out a low whistle. "Pretty impressive," he says. "What did you say your name was?"

"You didn't ask me. You asked my brother, because you assumed he was the only one here who mattered. My name is Andi." I stick out my hand. "Andi Kennedy."

His handshake is weak and clammy and sweaty. I love that I make him nervous.

Matthew clears his throat. "Well, Andi. Let me tell you what we're doing here this weekend. Mobilocity has teamed up with the festival to offer a contest for social media influencers. We're choosing five influencers to participate in a scavenger hunt through the festival for a chance to earn awesome Mobilocity prizes. And the grand prize winner gets an exclusive backstage interview with the Known before they headline the Main Stage on Sunday and an ongoing partnership with our brand. How does that sound?"

"It sounds like there's a catch," Jordan says.

"No catch." Hipster Matthew's eyes gleam as he strokes his beard. "All you have to do is post photos of all the scavenger hunt stops with the Mobilocity festival hashtag. Just share Mobilocity with your followers, and we'll share Mobilocity, and the Known, with you."

"Is this just for established influencers?" After the confidence I just pulled out for my sales pitch, I don't really want to admit that the only brand I have a sponsorship deal with is yarn. Will wanting to get to that level be enough to qualify me for this contest?

Matthew shakes his head. "Mobilocity is looking to make all kinds of connections this weekend. We love discovering new content."

This could be it. I want to do something with my channel that will launch its popularity. An exclusive interview with the Known. Go backstage at this famous music festival. Talk to one of the biggest bands in the world. Post it and get so many viewers. Subscribers. Ad revenue. And a partnership with Mobilocity means another income stream. Sure, it's not at all related to the channel I've been building, but do I care as long as it gets me to SCU?

"What does this entail?" I ask at the same time Jordan says, "Is it going to keep us from seeing the bands?"

"Not at all." Hipster Matthew leans across the card table, barely able to contain his excitement over giving us the scoop. "It's one event today, one event tomorrow, and one event on Sunday. I give everyone a clue, and you try to solve it as quickly as possible. But it's nothing major.

We want this to be a positive experience that you'll tell your followers about. We want you to enjoy the festival. That's why we're here."

There's no way I randomly stumbled on a way to solve all my problems after being on festival grounds for, like, five minutes. Could this really be legit? I peek at Jordan and raise my eyebrow. He crinkles his forehead and then his nose. I bite down on my bottom lip, and then he raises his eyebrow back. I love our twin facial recognition. It makes it so easy to communicate with each other in front of strangers. He thinks I could always sign up and then bail if it's dumb, and I agree with him.

"Where do I sign up?"

Hipster Matthew shoves a Mobilocity tablet at me. "Fill this out," he says. "Like I said, we're only taking five people, so we'll text you in about an hour to let you know if you're one of the lucky ones."

"It's not exactly crowded in here," Jordan jokes as I finish up the short online form.

"Well, the festival just opened," Hipster Matthew says. "And, look, there's someone now. Hey, guys, how are you doing?"

Once I'm finished, I drop the tablet on the table and turn around to see who is behind us.

And, of course, it's Jay Bankar. He's there with an older version of himself; I assume that's the mysterious dick brother who kept texting last night.

"You're a vlogger?" Jay sounds even more surprised than Hipster Matthew did earlier.

"I am."

"Don't sound so shocked," Jordan says. "Her channel is amazing."

"I'm not shocked," he says. "I just didn't know."

"I'm shocked," the brother says.

Jay elbows the brother. "God, shut up, Dev."

Hipster Matthew, who is not as oblivious as he first seemed to be, has caught on to the tension. "So, are you on the 'gram?" he says to Jay and his brother, moving in their direction. "We're looking for social media influencers . . ."

Hipster Matthew launches into his whole spiel, but I tune him out as I stare at Jay, who stares back with a look on his face. It's not the same friendly and charming expression from last night, nor is it the one of shock and hostility from earlier at the campsite. This is a look of respect.

"What's your channel all about?" Jay asks.

"Crafting," I say. "Go ahead and search it so you can make fun of it or prank me or whatever it is you do for laughs."

Understanding covers his face. "So that's what this is about. That's why you—"

"Want nothing to do with you? Yeah. I have zero desire to be part of whatever scheme or video you had planned for me. I've seen your videos, Jay Bankar. I think it's shady you didn't tell me who you were, I think it's shady you pulled some fake nice guy act, and I think it's shady you're standing there acting all surprised by this."

"Wow," he says. "You thought . . . wow. Okay, so that's not me."

"The guy in your videos isn't you?"

"Yes, that's me, but—" He rubs his hands over his face, like he's trying to wash something off. "It's not *me*."

"I don't know what you're talking about."

"It's not me for real. That's just a character. For the videos."

I ponder this for a second, wondering if he's being sincere or if this is a setup for some prank, and in that second, Hipster Matthew says "social media influencers" to Jay's brother about four more times.

"You're telling me you don't really do those things? Find unsuspecting people to prank and encourage your followers to make fun of them in the comments? Intentionally hurt people's feelings for sport? Make your own actual grandma think you might be dead?"

He shifts from foot to foot. "No, I mean—" He shoots a look at his brother, who is still listening to Hipster Matthew's sales pitch. Then something shifts in Jay's face. It hardens, and his face turns into the face I've seen on his videos. It's a totally different face, like he slipped on a Halloween mask. And I see in that moment what he meant about being different for the video. Being a character. Because he shifts into this face like you would slip into a new outfit, and the Jay I'd talked to the night before goes far, far away.

"So what if I do?" he says. "Everyone loves it. That's why the channel is called *You Know I'm Right*. I have the balls to say what you've been thinking."

That's always how he signs off his videos, and the sound of it live and in person makes my skin crawl.

"Well, what I know is right, Jay Bankar, is that you are the absolute worst. Please don't talk to me again." And I grab my brother by the arm and yank him out of the Mobilocity tent, hopefully leaving Jay Bankar behind forever.

CHAPTER 4

>>> • <<<

AN HOUR LATER, JORDAN AND I HAVE HIT UP A PIZZA stand called Spice Pie and each gobbled down a slice of pepperoni and jalapeño, which is officially the best thing I've ever eaten in my life. We also put down two bottles of water each because it's hot as balls out here, filmed some more festival B-roll, and caught the end of a set on the Desert Stage from a pretty awesome indie band we'd never heard of before called The Things They Buried. It's toward the end of their set that I get a text from Hipster Matthew.

> *You're in with Mobilocity! Meet in 15 minutes at the picture frame by the Cactus Stage for your Friday hunt. See you then! #MobilocityFamily*

I grab the side of Jordan's tank top and jump up and down. "We're in!" I'd been trying not to get too attached to this idea—that this contest and its incredible grand prize might be the thing to catapult me to YouTube fame and fortune, well, once I won and then filmed and edited it, anyway. But now that I hear that I'm in, I'm flooded with a feeling of rightness. I'm going to win this interview. It's going to change my life. And now with Jay Bankar in the mix, because, let's be real, they obviously chose him, too, pride is also on the line. There's no way I can let that asshat win.

After showing Jordan the text, we head out in search of the picture frame. Luckily the Desert Stage is right next to the Cactus Stage, so we don't have to go far to find the meeting spot. A large gilded frame is set up right in the middle of the grass, with a white canvas background a few feet behind, and people are posing for pictures inside of it. Jordan and I each take a few silly shots in the frame before scanning the crowd for Hipster Matthew. He has a Mobilocity flag stuck into the ground a few feet away, where he chats with a beautiful girl with long hair that starts black and ombres down to light brown and tan legs that are even longer.

"Oh, hey, you two," Hipster Matthew says in his fakey voice. "This is Sadie Díaz. She's one of the other competitors today."

Sadie smiles at us, and my brother momentarily morphs into the human version of the heart eyes emoji. I don't blame him, honestly. I'm about to get a case of the goo-goo eyes myself. It's a thousand degrees out here, and sweat is pouring off me in buckets, but this girl has the most perfect makeup I have ever seen in my life. Her face looks like it should be on a poster or in a magazine, not standing in front of me in real life. Her clothes, too, are straight off of some "How to Dress at a Summer Music Festival" *BuzzFeed* list, while mine are damp and probably smelly and sticking to me in awkward places. How is she so sweat-free? And will she share her secrets?

"Hey, Sadie," I say. "I'm Andi, and this is my brother, Jordan. How did you qualify to get drawn into Matthew's evil web?"

Sadie smiles back. "Oh, I just do makeup tutorials for fun," she says, twisting the ends of a piece of hair around her fingers. "It's no big deal." Ah, that makes sense. No wonder she looks so perfect. It's pretty much her job. "What about you?"

"I have a YouTube channel," I say. "About crafting." I hate the way the words come out of my mouth, like I'm trying to swallow them back before they can escape. Unlike the confidence I pulled out when trying to pitch myself to Hipster Matthew, this time I sound small. Like what I'm doing doesn't matter. Sadie's perfect face has knocked me completely off-kilter.

"So, which bands are you excited about this weekend?" Nothing like a little music talk to get my confidence back. "Have you heard of the band the Gold Parade? They're playing later. They're from Pasadena, where we're from. You should check them out. They're really good."

Now it's Sadie who looks a little out of her element. "I don't know too much about most of the bands here. I'm not really a music person."

My eyes bug out, and I'm sure Jordan's do, too. "Not a music person? How . . . what?" I say at the same time Jordan asks, "What are you even doing here, then?"

"Sorry about my brother." I deliver a swift blow to Jordan's ribs, and he doubles over in mock agony. "We just come from a long line of music fans. Our dad was a radio DJ, so not being music people wasn't really an option in our home."

Sadie shrugs. "Well, it's Cabazon, right? Why not? My friends had an extra ticket, it seemed fun, and I can do some fun festival looks for my channel. It's not like I had anything else going on this weekend."

I'm about to serve up a list of bands that she might like to try out when I'm interrupted by Hipster Matthew. "Okay, peeps. Everyone is here."

I was so caught up in my conversation with Sadie, I didn't notice everyone else had shown up, including Jay Bankar and Brother Bankar. God, did Jay really have to wear that tank top? It's like he's rubbing those biceps in my face on purpose.

Hipster Matthew pulls out his phone, the latest Mobilocity release, I'm sure, and points the screen toward himself. "Welcome to Mobilocity! And welcome to Cabazon!" he says to the camera before turning it to face us. "It's time for a Mobilocity scavenger hunt with some of our favorite social media influencers. Here's the deal. There are five of you competing over the course of the weekend. We chose you folks because you all cover a wide range of demographics, content areas, and geographical locations. Mobilocity is an up-and-coming brand, so we're excited to partner with some up-and-coming creators."

"AKA more reach for their advertising," I whisper to Jordan, and he laughs.

"We have Sadie from San Diego, who is a beauty influencer; Andi and her crafting channel from LA; Quan from San Francisco on Twitch; Cody from Phoenix with a book podcast; and Jay, also from LA, who has a lifestyle channel."

I try to keep my scoff from being audible. Lifestyle channel? If being a public jerkoff is a lifestyle, well, that's pretty sad.

"There will be three scavenger hunt tasks." Hipster Matthew turns the camera back toward himself and runs his free hand over his beard. "One per day. The first person to complete the task wins five points and the daily prize. The second person wins four points, the third person wins three points, etc. The goal, obviously, is to finish first and win the points. The person with the most points after task three wins the grand prize—an exclusive backstage interview with the Known before they headline the festival on Sunday, a brand-new Mobilocity tablet to help with all of your social media needs, and a brand partnership."

As Hipster Matthew explains the rules to the camera, I eyeball the competition.

Quan is a tall Asian guy with spiky black hair and a T-shirt with some video game joke on it that I don't get. He has a big smile on his face, though, and he exudes chill.

I'm not sure if Cody is the guy or girl standing next to Quan. They're a cute Black couple, holding hands, and they're wearing even cuter matching T-shirts that say GOOD BOOKS AND GOOD GRAMMAR, which I assume is the name of the podcast.

Then there's gorgeous Sadie, who chews on her manicured thumbnail as she listens to Hipster Matthew, and Jerky Jay, who, as I turn to peek at him, seems to be looking at me already.

We make eye contact.

He smiles.

I scowl.

Hipster Matthew turns the camera back to us, panning to each of our faces. "Today's scavenger hunt game is Cabazon Festival Bingo. You'll each get a card of things or people you need to find here on the festival grounds, photograph, and upload to at least one of your public social channels with the hashtags for the festival and the competition. The picture has to have you in it. We need proof you actually took the picture and didn't steal it from someone else's feed. Cheating won't be tolerated, so don't even try it, or we'll kick you out." An enormous smile spreads behind his beard. "Okay, is everyone ready to party?"

Sadie lets out a loud whoop, while the rest of us clap with various levels of enthusiasm.

"All right, let's do this," he says into the camera. "I'll pass out the bingo cards, and the first one back here with one row completed and pictures uploaded and hashtagged on social media is the winner of five points and our first prize, a rad pair of Mobilocity noise-canceling headphones."

I pull out my phone and make sure it's on. I generally don't turn my phone off ever, but with limited battery-charging opportunities out here in the desert, I'm trying to be as conservative as possible.

"Oh, yeah, one last thing. I have Mobilocity phones for all of you to use on this task. These brand-new Mobilocity Ninja X phones are connected to our secure festival Wi-Fi and have a freshly charged battery just for this task. And if you folks want, you can leave your own phones here, no matter what brand they are, and I can charge them for you at our charging station." He puts his own phone in his pocket and pulls five new phones out of his Mobilocity-branded messenger bag. The sun glints off of their sleek silver casings, and my fingers itch to grab one and start poking around.

"Every app you'll need is on there, so take a minute and get signed on to anything you're going to use. And, of course, we encourage you all to tweet, Instagram, Snapchat, Facebook, YouTube, TikTok, whatever, as you go through the hunt. Tell all your friends and followers all about what you're up to!"

"Just make sure you mention Mobilocity!" Jordan whispers as I sign into Instagram, and I snicker.

Once we're signed in and I've handed my own phone and both my portable chargers over for a good charging, we're ready to go. All of us contestants share nervous glances back and forth. None of us are really sure how to interact with one another while we wait for Hipster Matthew to come back from the charging station. Are we friends? Enemies? Frenemies? I certainly want to push Jay off the side of the earth, but I'm not sure about the rest of them just yet.

"Sooo . . . ," I say, eager to break the somewhat awkward silence. "Which bands are you all checking out later?"

Sadie shrugs. Quan and the podcasting couple Cody and Corey (with their unisex names, I'm not sure which one is which and I feel weird asking, so I mentally call them the Cs) mention a few of the super-popular bands playing on Sunday right before the headliners.

"I'm amped about this band called the Gold Parade later today," Jay says. "They're from Pasadena. You've probably heard of them." He gives me this look like we're sharing some kind of inside joke that makes me want to smack that sparkling grin off his face.

"Oh!" Sadie says. "Andi was actually just telling me about that band!"

Jay is saved from a biting sarcastic comment, which I hadn't actually planned out just yet but which was sure to decimate him, by Hipster Matthew's return from the charging station.

"Okay, team. Is everyone ready? Phones on and signed in?"

We all confirm we're ready, so he hands us our bingo cards, facedown. "Don't turn them over until I tell you to. Gotta get this on video." He pulls out his own phone again, pointing it toward us. "Okay, let's do this. First team back here with bingo is the winner. Everyone set? Annnnnd . . . go."

We all flip over our cards, which look like typical bingo cards with things we might see at the festival filling each of the squares and *Selfie* right in the middle as the free square. The smart thing to do would be to make some kind of plan of action but (a) I want to get away from the rest of the group as quickly as possible, and (b) my eyes zero in on one we can get right away.

"'Band with at least five words in their name,'"

I whisper to Jordan. "Still Standing at the End of the World is playing at the Cactus Stage right now. I saw them on our way over here. Let's do this one before anyone else figures it out."

Jordan nods, and we're off, though we take a circular route to the closer Cactus Stage in an attempt to throw everyone off.

Still Standing at the End of the World isn't my normal fare; they're a little too screamy for me, but I do have them on a few playlists, and I recognized them immediately when we walked by earlier. They have a solid crowd, so Jordan and I creep up the side of the tent until we're close to the stage but far on the side. The second the black-haired lead singer climbs up on the front speaker to scream into the mic, Jordan snaps a picture of me giving a thumbs-up with them in the background.

"You upload and hashtag," I say. "I'll figure out our next spot." Now that we've committed to one of the squares, our path from here is limited if we want to get bingo. "Okay, one of these lines has 'couple making out.' That's not a challenge."

"The beer garden is right across the way," Jordan says as he taps on the phone. "I bet we'd be able to find a few of those over there."

A tall white guy with muscles spilling out of his too-tight polo shirt stands by the opening to the gated beer garden checking IDs, so we obviously can't get in, but that's okay. It's enclosed by a chain-link fence, and we can see into it just fine. Including the couple lying flat on the ground practically mounting each other right up against the fence.

"Yikes," I say as I pose by the fence, with the, uh, amorous couple in the background. You can't see their faces at all, which is good, but you can definitely tell they check off our box. Jordan uploads the picture, and I can't help but smile at the fact that it's been less than ten minutes and we already have two of the pictures done. I doubt the other teams have been this successful already.

Jordan takes the bingo card from me and runs his finger down it. "We're pretty committed to this row now."

"Oh God," I say, scanning the rest of the squares. "We really should have planned this out better. 'Ride on the Ferris wheel' will be easy, but it's all the way on the other side of the grounds, and there will be a line. 'Moving piece of art' shouldn't be too hard. There must be one somewhere, we'll just have to find it. We can be on the lookout when we go over to the Ferris wheel. But celebrity? That's the hardest one on here. How are we going to find a celebrity just walking around?"

"Does someone onstage count? Some of these singers are pretty famous."

"No, there's an asterisk. See?" I point at the small print at the bottom of the card. "'Celebrity can't be on a stage.' This is going to be tough."

"We'll figure it out," Jordan says. "Let's head over to the Ferris wheel right now and keep our eyes peeled for moving art and famous people."

We take off across the manicured grass, dodging wandering festivalgoers, none of whom appear to be famous, and art installations, none of which seem to be moving.

When we arrive, there's a short line at the giant Ferris wheel that towers over the festival. We hop into line, and I shift nervously from foot to foot. "We should have done one of the other rows. We could have easily gotten glow sticks at the Palm Tree Stage. It's a big rave in there."

"Don't worry," Jordan says. "We'll figure it out."

I tap on the shoulders of the couple in front of me. "Hey, have you two seen any celebrities here today?"

"Nah," the guy says, shaking his head.

I turn to the people behind us in line and ask the same question but get a similar reply.

"I mean, who's to say who's a celebrity?" I scratch my head as I scan the crowd, hoping to see a face I recognize. "Someone might be famous to me, but someone else has never even heard of them. Sadie just heard about the Gold Parade an hour ago, but I would die if their lead singer walked by right now."

"Who knows," Jordan says, shrugging. "Sadie might even be a celebrity in the makeup world."

"Ooh, let's look her up." Our line is inching along, so we have time to do a little research on the competition.

Jordan types her name in the search bar, and my mouth falls open. "Oh my God, look how many subscribers she has. That's bonkers." She has over five hundred thousand followers for her very professional-looking YouTube channel. "Jeez, she said this was no big deal. She's totally a big deal." I'm about to tap on one of the videos and see what it is she does to get so much traffic when I hear some familiar voices run by us.

Jay and his brother.

"Hurry up, Jay," Dev snaps at his brother as they rush by. Jay rolls his eyes as he trails behind.

I elbow Jordan, and we try to melt into the line and be invisible as best we can. We don't want them to know where we are or how we're doing at all, even though I'm dying to get a good peek at their bingo card. I guess we could go on Jay's photo feed and spy on what he's posted. I grab the phone from Jordan's hand so I can check up on them, but it fumbles out of my fingers and drops to the ground. "Crap."

And, of course, Jay hears me. And looks. And stops. Double crap.

He looks from me to his brother to me again. Then, with a strange expression on his face, he runs up to where we're waiting in line. In a whisper that tumbles from his mouth so quickly I almost can't catch it, he says, "Lukas MacDonald is sitting on a red blanket with his girlfriend toward the back of the Main Stage crowd."

Then, without waiting for a reply, he turns back toward his brother and runs off.

My brother gapes at me while I stare after Jay's retreating form. "Did he just tell us where we can find a celebrity?"

I nod, but I'm baffled. I think that's what happened? Sure, it makes sense that Lukas MacDonald, former Disney Channel golden boy and current tabloid fodder, would be at a festival like this one, but . . .

"Why would Jay help us?"

Jordan shrugs. "No idea."

"Unless it's a trick. That's his thing. Maybe he's setting us up for some prank."

"But filming a prank on us would take time out from him winning. That doesn't make sense."

"Nothing he's done so far makes sense," I say, and I chew on my thumbnail the rest of the time we wait in the line, trying to figure out what the heck Jay Bankar's endgame is.

A minute or two later, it's our turn to board the Ferris wheel. We take time to enjoy the beautiful view of the festival below us by shooting some more B-roll. The stages, all of which we can see from here, the campsite, which is even bigger and more expansive than we realized, the rows and rows of cars of the people who drove into the festival. Beyond all of it lies the beautiful California desert, tall palm trees, then craggy hills, then blue, blue sky, stretching out for miles.

At the top of the Ferris wheel, I shift over so the view of the festival is behind me, and Jordan snaps a picture. For the first time since Jordan told me about the tickets, I feel like I can relax and just enjoy the experience for a moment. I clear my head of everything—this video I can't figure out, Dad, college, money, and the newest thorn in my side, Jay Bankar, who seems to be dancing around the edge of every thought I've had since I first laid eyes on him. I push all of it out the side of the Ferris wheel car and close my eyes, breathing in the desert air. It's peaceful here, with a slight breeze blowing and the gentle rocking of the car as the wheel drops us and then pulls us up again.

What would it be like to just be able to have fun here? Watch our favorite bands and eat pizza and dance and sing without stressing about filming a video? Enjoy this time with Jordan without thinking that we might not have chances like this next year? Just hang out without worrying about a contest and hashtags?

Just be able to flirt with the cute guy at the campsite across the way without him being so damn problematic?

The thought of all of it is so peaceful, so meditative, I almost doze off.

But we don't get a chance to enjoy the sleepy peace for too long, because soon our car is back down at the bottom and it's time for us to snap back into reality, hop out, and get back to our hunt.

"So, what do you think?" Jordan asks. "The Main Stage is right here. Should we go check it out? See if we can find Lukas MacDonald?"

It doesn't make sense for Jay to help us, but I also don't see why he would bother to go out of his way to trick us if he couldn't film it for his channel. I shrug. "We have nothing else to go on right now, do we? Let's go."

We take off in a jog toward the back of the Main Stage crowd, where people are spread out on blankets, towels, and sweatshirts watching Queenie, a sixteen-year-old breakout singer and guitar player. She's ridiculously talented, but a little more poppy than the music I usually listen to.

We scan the blankets for a red one. I'm about to declare this tip a dud and figure Jay was trying to send us off on a bad clue so he could have more time to win, when I spot it. A red blanket occupied by a white guy in a baseball cap and an Asian girl with her black hair pulled into a messy topknot.

I elbow Jordan, and we casually creep up to the blanket, trying, and probably failing, to be inconspicuous. When we get to the side, it's pretty clear the guy sitting there is definitely Lukas MacDonald, former child star of many shows on the Disney network. He was in the news recently for checking into the hospital for exhaustion, which Mom told us is definitely celebrity code for drugs.

Unbelievable. Jay was being straight with us. Lukas MacDonald is here, right where Jay said he would be.

My stomach squeezes slightly at the thought of taking Lukas MacDonald's picture and putting it online. I have a personal rule about that, but the fine print is a little loose when it comes to celebrities. Yeah, I could ask him to pose, but he seems to be enjoying himself. I don't want to bother him. Taking a photo without him knowing makes me feel a little bit like Jay, but I'm not doing it to make fun of him, so it's okay, right?

Now Jordan elbows me and mouths, *Hurry up*, and I realize that I'm not going to win this interview if I don't take this photo, so I push all the squicky feelings aside and squat down near the red blanket putting my hands out like I'm presenting something while Jordan snaps a picture. I check out the picture to make sure you can tell it's an actual celebrity, and, yup, you can definitely tell that's Lukas MacDonald. No matter how much he tries to shed that Disney image, that baby face and those dimples are forever.

I take a quick glance around one more time to make sure Jay isn't lurking behind someone, ready to jump out and prank us somehow. But he's not. This was actually legit.

He helped us.

Jordan uploads the picture while I make a mental note

to delete it once this whole thing is over, then he tugs on the hem of my shirt. "Okay, one more square."

"Oh, yeah. Moving art. Moving how? What does this even mean?"

"No idea."

"Well, let's head back to the frame and ask people along the way. Someone has to know what this clue means."

We're off on a jog again, dodging drunks and weirdos and stopping to ask anyone who seems seminormal if they can help us in our quest.

"Hey," I say to a nice-looking group of ladies who must be in their thirties. I kinda love that they are here at this festival. I hope I'm still having fun at concerts when I'm married and have kids and stuff. "Have you seen a piece of art that's moving? We're trying to win a scavenger hunt."

We've already asked three groups of people with no luck. If these women can't help us, I'm going to have to start wandering into the crowds watching the bands or talk to every single person waiting in line for Spice Pie. There are dozens of pieces of random art—sculptures, structures, paintings, statues—throughout this festival. Someone has to have seen one of the damn things moving around.

Recognition crosses the faces of all the women immediately, and they all laugh. Loudly. "We saw it, all right," the tallest white lady says from underneath her enormous straw hat, which makes the others laugh even more. There is obviously some sort of story there. I wish I had time to hear it, because the way the tall one is turning red, it's obviously a good one.

"Do you mind telling us where?" Jordan says in his flirting-with-older-ladies voice. "We're kind of in a hurry."

"Oh, yeah," the shortest white lady says. "Sorry, we . . . never mind. It's over there." She points to the tent in the middle of the polo field that has been set up as a bit of an outdoor DJ dance party. "On the other side of that tent there's a big hand. The fingers move around on their own."

"Well," a Black woman in a caftan says, "they make it seem like they move on their own. But there's clearly someone controlling them from somewhere. As we learned." The women dissolve into laughter again.

The second they tell us where to go, we're on the move. "Thank you," I shout from over my shoulder.

"Good luck," they shout back. "Watch out for those fingers."

"I'm glad I didn't hear that story," Jordan says as we weave through the dance party tent.

"Are you kidding? I totally wanted to hear the rest."

I see it the second we step out of the dance party tent. It's a hand made out of something that resembles chicken wire that stands about ten feet in the air. It's on a flat base and doesn't appear to be moving at first, but then, slowly, the wrist rotates and the thumb straightens out on the side, so it looks like it's giving a big high five.

Perfect. I can't see who is operating it or how, but all I care about is the fact that it's moving.

"Okay," I say to my brother. "Let's get a quick picture of me in front of it, and we'll be done."

"Hmm," he says. "Do you think it will count if we just get a picture? Can you tell it's moving?"

"Good point," I say. "Let's not chance it. Do a Boomerang."

I stand in front of the hand right as the fingers start shifting around, and, since it's a Boomerang, I hop back and forth, praying the hand behind me is moving in a convincing way.

Jordan puts the phone down after a few seconds, his face bright red, and he lets out a laugh so loud it shakes his entire body. "Those women weren't kidding. There is definitely someone running that hand somewhere." He hands me the phone and taps PLAY. Behind my silly dance, the fingers rearrange themselves until they're all folded down. Except the middle one.

"It's flipping us off!" I yell. "Oh my God!" I turn to look at the hand, but it's all cables and metal. I can see right through it to the other side, and I have no idea where anyone could be hiding to work the controls. Unbelievable.

"I love you, too!" I yell to the hand. Jordan uploads the Boomerang, which I know is going to be a hit to my followers and anyone else checking out this hashtag, and he smiles at me. "We're done," he says. "Let's go."

The two of us run as fast as we can manage back to the frame, dodging people at every turn. Hipster Matthew is standing by the Mobilocity banner playing on his phone.

"He's alone," I say, smacking my brother on the arm. "Do you think we beat everyone?"

"Dude, I think so," Jordan says. We run faster.

"Matthew!" I yell as we approach. "We're here!"

Matthew looks up from his phone with a big smile. "Rad," he says. "Let me see your bingo card and your photo feed."

I unfold the card from my back pocket, and Jordan hands him our phone. He scrolls through it, smiling. "Okay, we have moving artwork. Nice Boomerang, by the way. Who is this? Lukas MacDonald? Wow. Where was he?"

"Over by the Main Stage," I said, waving my hand for him to hurry up and check us.

"We thought that one would be pretty difficult. I'm impressed." He looks back at the phone. "Okay, Ferris wheel. Oooh, nice capture. Couple making out. And what band is this?"

"Still Standing at the End of the World," I say, running my hand through my hair. God, is he going to ask about the filter of each one, too?

"Nice," he says, handing us the phone back. "But you missed one."

"What? No, we didn't." I snatch the card from him and trace my finger across the line. "We got all of them."

"You didn't do the middle one." And he points to the freebie spot in the middle of the bingo card, which, after all of this, is still unchecked.

Oh my God, I can't believe I missed the stupid middle square. Well, I didn't miss it. I saw it and laughed at it and then immediately skipped over it because it was so ridiculous.

Selfie.

I scramble to grab the phone from Jordan and point it at myself, and right as I do, I see Jay and his brother run up behind me in the front-facing camera.

CHAPTER 5

>>> • <<<

"SHIT," I SAY, AND I SNAP THE MOST UNFLATTERING
selfie I've ever taken. I usually take a few before I post,
analyzing lighting and angles for the best one. But I don't
have time to be that serious about posting a bad photo
right now. I have this one picture, where I'm making the
derpiest face and my entire forehead is wrinkled up and
my nose looks crooked, and I have the team I want more
than anything to lose running up to beat me right there
in the background.

I suck it up and upload the awful photo, quickly add-
ing all the appropriate hashtags, of course. I'll go back
later and add a funny caption or something.

I shove the phone at Hipster Matthew at the very
moment Jay and Dev Bankar run up to the Mobilocity
banner.

I did it. I got it in first.

I won. I beat Jay Bankar.

It takes everything inside of me to stay put and not to

leap into the air and rub this victory in his stupid, hot face.

Winning this contest, this interview, might have seemed like a total long shot at first, but now I have one win under my belt, and it's becoming more real. From a hazy mirage off in the distance to something with a distinct shape and edges. A place I can actually get to.

"Hey, guys," Hipster Matthew says to them. "You're the second team to arrive today. Let me check your pictures in a sec." He turns to me, waving the phone with my god-awful selfie still on the screen, and smiles. "Five points to Andi, who is on her way to winning the interview with the Known," he says. "And the first day prize, this pair of rad Mobilocity Bluetooth earbuds."

"Sweet," Jordan says, grabbing at the box.

"Mine," I say to him, winking.

"What?" Dev Bankar literally stomps his foot on the ground, which is not something I have ever seen anyone but my four-year-old cousin do when he doesn't get a second cookie. Dev has got to be at least twenty, but he looks like he's five seconds away from a temper tantrum. "How did they win? There's no way. They must have cheated or something. We were so fast."

Jay's eyes drill holes in the ground. His brother has no idea Jay told us where to find Lukas MacDonald, and from his brother's reaction to their loss, I can see why. Dev Bankar isn't exactly winning any sportsmanship awards.

So why did Jay help us, then? He wasn't just putting his own chances at winning at risk by giving us that information, he was also risking getting on his brother's shit list. Given what Dev has shown of his winning personality so far, that second one is probably worse, honestly.

Finally, Jay looks up at me. I try to figure out what's on his face, but I can't decipher it. The only face of his I'm really used to is his smarmy online video face; this honest expression takes me by surprise. With no one else around, this might be a good time to talk to him. Try to get a little insight into what's going on in that head of his. But before I can, Sadie runs up, with Cody and Corey not far behind her. Hipster Matthew doles out the points. Four for Jay, three for Sadie, two for the Cs. One point for Quan when he finally gets here.

Hipster Matthew congratulates us and insists on taking a group photo on each of our individual cameras and watching while we post them to our own feeds. "You won't get your own phones back from the charging station until you do," he says in this voice that's trying for joking but says *my job is on the line here* instead. I have no doubt he would hold our own phones hostage until we did his Mobilocity hashtag bidding.

The whole time I am aggressively avoiding eye contact with Jay Bankar. I can feel his eyes on me, but I focus my gaze on the grass or Cody's and Corey's matching T-shirts, or I watch my brother drool over Sadie. But I don't let myself give in to the curiosity to see what it is Jay is staring at or why.

Hipster Matthew tells us to meet up at the same place, same time tomorrow for round two, and trots off to grab our phones from the secret charging station. It's been about an hour since we started. I was worried this whole scavenger hunt situation would take too much time away from the festival and make me miss some of the bands I was looking forward to, but we've hardly missed anything and we're on the way to winning the interview. I don't want to spend too much time thinking about how *easy* this all seems so far, because I know those thoughts will immediately jinx it all, but is this really all it takes? Step 1: show up. Step 2: kick butt. Step 3: profit. Could it all come together so smoothly and end with me getting everything I want? The thought makes me giddy, like I'm getting away with something huge, like robbing a bank. And now Jordan and I have the rest of the afternoon and evening free to enjoy the bands. And get more Spice Pie.

Mom's voice pops into my head, though, telling me that I better come up with a backup plan, just in case, and, much like actual Mom, that voice of hers in my head is usually right. I turn to Jordan to plan the rest of our day, but he has sidled over to Sadie and started chatting her up.

"Ugh," I say under my breath. I don't begrudge my

brother some flirting, especially with Sadie, who is gorgeous. And even if I did begrudge him, that wouldn't stop him. A tornado plowing through this festival wouldn't stop him. I just wish he would not flirt with the competition and would at least wait until I don't need to talk to him.

Apparently my sound of annoyance was actually audible, because just as sneakily as Jordan sidled up to Sadie, Jay has sidled up to me.

"Does he do this often?" he asks.

"What do you mean?" I snap. *I'm* allowed to talk shit about my twin brother. No one else is allowed to talk shit about my twin brother.

"Well," he says, "last night he left you alone in the dark to set up your tent, right?"

I don't give him the satisfaction of a response. Last night with Jay already seems so long ago, or like an out-of-body experience, or like it was a weird dream that is already slipping from my memory like a mist. He was a totally different person, and I'm pissed at him for reminding me of who he could have been. I liked that guy, damn it.

"And now, not even twenty-four hours later, he's set his sights on someone new. You were clearly annoyed last night, and you're clearly annoyed now. So it seems like it's a thing. That you're always trying to keep him in line and he just does what he wants. Right?"

"What the hell? You don't know anything about either of us," I snap again. "I'd appreciate it if you stopped acting like you did." Being snarky is so foreign to me, and I'm disappointed that I couldn't come up with a more biting response. The perfect witty reply will probably pop into my head in about four hours, when it's way too late. It's Jordan who always thinks up good comebacks on the fly. Too bad he's otherwise engaged.

And the reason I need a witty comeback in the first place.

Jay's mouth twitches. "Look, Andi," he says, stepping toward me and lowering his voice. "I'm sorry we took a wrong turn somewhere. I don't—"

"It wasn't a wrong turn," I say. "I never would have talked to you if I'd realized who you were. I would have rather slept in my car than let Jay Bankar help me for a single second."

He lets out a long sigh. Given what I know about him, I'm surprised he hasn't pushed back at me. Snapped, snarked, or given me shit in return. He seems determined to make me like him. Too bad. So much effort for something that is so never going to happen.

"Why do you hate me so much?"

"Oh, let me see. You seek out people to act nice to only to prank them, laugh at them, and then humiliate them on your channel. You think your pranks are funny, but you're just tricking someone into showing actual, real feelings over something and then you're making fun of them for having those feelings. It's manipulative, and it's mocking people for trusting you and having emotions. It's disgusting. And you know I'm right. I have the balls to say what everyone has been thinking." I shouldn't let on that I've watched his videos that much, but I can't help but use his tagline against him. I don't watch them because I enjoy them. I hate-watch them. I watch them when I need to redirect some anger toward something.

"Okay, but—"

"No, I'm not done. You put down women on your channel, and that's gross. I have nothing to say to someone who—what did you say?—thinks any chick who doesn't find you hilarious is too stupid to live? Weren't those your exact words?"

He runs his hand through his hair and stares off at the distance. Then he turns toward his brother, who has wandered a few feet away to do something on the loaner phone, and a darkness crosses his face. He scoots closer.

"That's my brother," he says quietly.

"What?"

"Quiet, okay?" He lowers his voice more, so it's almost a whisper. "It's my brother. On the videos."

He's obviously not being literal here, but I glance from Jay to Dev and back to Jay again, just to check. They look similar, I guess. But aside from being older, Dev looks like an indoor guy, while Jay is clearly athletic. Plus, Dev has scruffy facial hair and this odd way about him, like he doesn't interact with other human beings much.

"Don't try to pull that crap with me, Jay. I've seen your videos. I'm not an idiot, so don't act like—"

He puts his hand up to stop me. "I can't talk about this now." He glances nervously back toward his brother, who has finished his internetting and is walking back toward the group. "Can we just meet for the Gold Parade like we planned? I want to explain. And . . ."

"And what?"

He shrugs. "I liked hanging out with you last night, that's all. I'd love a second chance."

Despite myself, despite the fact that I don't give second chances to anyone but Jordan, who continually craps all over them, a small spark of curiosity lights up deep inside of me. There's something about Jay's shrug and his open expression that cracks my shell the tiniest bit, and it twists me all up inside to realize how intrigued I am. He doesn't know that I'm a sucker for a good story, and I always have been. That I'd hang on to every word of my dad's radio interviews, engrossed in all the wild tales these musicians and celebrities would tell, even when I didn't understand half of what they were talking about. Obsessed with his man-on-the-street interviews, where people shared wild, wacky stories about their personal lives. So, even though there is a loud, sensible part of me worrying that this might be one of Jay's pranks, it can't manage to talk sense into that other part of me who can't stop wondering about the story he has to tell me.

How maybe this awful person he is on YouTube really *isn't* him.

"Look," I say, "I'm going to be at the Gold Parade. Somewhere. Maybe I'll see you. Maybe I won't. Okay?" I cross my arms tightly across my chest, and I also try to scowl, but I'm not really the scowling type, so I have no idea what it actually looks like on my face.

"I'll take it," he says. And he breaks out into this huge, wide-open grin. I've never seen a smile like it on any of his videos I've hate-watched. I didn't even see such a big smile on him last night when we were hanging out, before any of this other crap got in the way.

I feel a tingle under my skin at that smile.

Stop it, Andi. This guy is bad news. Don't fall for the smile.

But the tingle doesn't listen.

"Can I ask you why you did it, though?"

He looks at me, puzzled.

"Lukas MacDonald?"

He shakes his head and jerks it in the direction of his brother. "We'll talk at the Gold Parade, okay?"

I nod, my curiosity getting the better of me. Something is obviously up with those Bankar brothers.

Finally, Hipster Matthew returns with our fully charged phones. He hands them out, reminds us about tomorrow's meeting time, aggressively encourages us to continue to tag our photos with the Mobilocity hashtag, and tells us to have a "rad" rest of the day at the festival.

Before Jay Bankar can get under my skin any more, I grab Jordan by the shirt and drag him away from the group.

"That's strike two," I say to him as we walk toward the center of the festival.

"Strike two on what?"

"Ditching me this weekend to flirt with a girl."

"I didn't ditch you," he says, indignant. "I was standing right there."

"You can't just run off and leave me alone with Jay Bankar. That's not cool, man. You're my brother. I need you to protect me from getting harassed by assholes."

"Assholes? I saw you talking to him, and you were smiling. An actual grin. It didn't seem like you were being harassed at all."

Ugh. I guess I didn't even get close to a scowl. Damn. "The smile was a lie," I say. "You know me, I smile at everyone."

"So, if I see you hugging him . . . ?"

"I will never hug him." The memory of last night's awkward hug shoots a tingle up and down my body. I hugged him without even thinking about it then, and that brief physical contact with him lit me up like fireworks on the Fourth of July. Damn, he has such a good body under that tank top. It's so unfair. "Well, I might hug him. But the hug will be a lie. He's an ass."

Jordan stops walking and stares at me. The twin stare. The *you're feeding me some bullshit, and you forget that I know you better than anyone else* stare.

God, I hate that stare.

"What?" I narrow my eyes at him.

He shrugs and laughs. "Nothing. I just know you, that's all."

"What do you know?"

"I know you don't hate this guy as much as you want to think you do."

His statement strikes a chord in me. On some level, I wonder if he's right, because there seem to be two Jays. There's awful internet Jay and this real life Jay who has been nothing but nice to me. He helped me build my tent and went out of his way to drop a clue for the scavenger hunt, and he has kept trying to be nice even though I've given him no reason to do so. I am having a hard time reconciling these two very different people in my head.

"Where was your twin telepathy when I was stranded in the dark with the tent last night? I was definitely using it to send a few choice words your way."

"Bad reception, I guess. No service out here in the desert." Jordan throws his arm around my neck and playfully pulls me into him. "So, are we going to see a band, or what? I think Into the Mist is on at the Desert Stage in about twenty minutes. I really liked their latest album."

"Fine," I say. "But I think it might be time for—"

"If you aren't going to say more Spice Pie, don't even bother finishing your sentence."

"Well, I was going to say it's time to make a game plan for this video. But we can discuss that over Spice Pie, for sure."

We reroute ourselves toward the nearest Spice Pie stand. We've seen several during our run around the festival grounds, which is a good thing, and drool pools up in my mouth the second the smell of fresh pizza wafts toward my nostrils.

"So, what is there to even discuss?" Jordan says as he steps into the long line and I fall in next to him. "You're going to win this contest and interview the Known as your festival video. And then Mom's head will explode. Not only because of how many views an interview with such a huge band will get you, but because she's all hot for Bernard White. She still talks about that selfie she took with him when Dad interviewed the Known for the radio station. Remember how she swore he flirted with her, even though Dad was right there?"

"Well, obviously I'm hoping that's how it will go. The interview, I mean, not the flirting. But what if it doesn't?"

"You don't need that kind of negativity in your life."

I step up on my toes to see how many people are in front of us in line. Spice Pie is obviously popular; its line is twice as long as any of the other food stands surrounding it. "Why do you think this is so delicious? I've had pizza with jalapeños on it before, and it was never this good."

"The people making it are probably high. Maybe they drop drugs into the crust or something?"

I know Jordan is kidding, but we really have run through our fair share of smoke clouds that were not just the cigarette variety. And our neighbors at the campsite with the constant dance party? They never went to sleep, if you know what I mean.

"Anyway, I'm not being negative, I'm being practical. I could lose. What do I do then?"

"Honestly, I'm surprised you haven't come up with something yet. You're never at a loss for video ideas."

He's right. I've been filming crafting videos for my channel for over a year now, and something new is always getting me excited to create. I have a long list of ideas for future crafts in a special hand-decorated notebook that I actually made for one of my very first videos. Friendship bracelets is currently circled, but I never actually finished the video I was working on when Jordan told me about the festival, so I haven't crossed it off and moved to one of the six or seven ideas listed under it yet.

So it's not that ideas in general elude me, it's just that

my brain naturally directs itself toward potential crafts, like some kind of self-driving car. Nothing else is getting me excited, not even something music-related, which is my other big love.

"I know I was all on board with fashion or band interviews or something, but . . ." I trail off because I'm not sure how to explain to Jordan this pit in my stomach. Sure, I could abandon crafts and focus on something else that would bring more of an audience. I could turn my back on my small group of loyal subscribers in favor of a potentially larger audience. I could take a total 180 from what drew me to making videos and posting them online in the first place. But all of that would be like tossing everything that makes me who I am, and everything that I want to be, into a dumpster and setting it on fire.

It's exactly how I feel when I think about Jordan going to SCU without me next year. I could go to a different school and get a good education. I could save some money at a community college for two years and transfer. I do have other options.

But this school is my connection to Dad. And to Mom. And as much as I act like I want to punt him across this polo field, I'm not ready to leave my brother. I may have been rankled by Jay's joke about trying to keep Jordan in line, but, come on, look at him. My brother needs me. How is he going to keep his shit together if I'm not there to help him?

We reach the front of the line before I have a chance to unpack my suitcase of feelings, and we order two Spice Pies and two sodas, then walk with our food back over to the Desert Stage for Into the Mist.

"He says it's his brother," I say.

"Whaa?" Jordan's mouth is full of pizza. I guess I should have waited until he finished his food.

"Jay Bankar. When I called him out on being awful in his videos, he said it's his brother, not him."

"Of course it's him. What does that even mean?" We stand at the back of the crowd under the tent at the Desert Stage while we finish our Spice Pie and wait for the band to go on.

"I don't know. Last night we talked about going to see the Gold Parade together. He asked me to come by so we could finish the conversation." I shrug. "He wouldn't finish there because his brother walked up."

"Sounds like his brother has him by the balls." Jordan shoves the rest of the pizza in his mouth and wipes his face with a napkin. "Are you going to go?"

"I don't know. I mean, I'm going to the Gold Parade for sure, but I guess I'll see how I feel about talking to him in a few hours." I finish up my pizza, too, and toss my greasy plate and crumpled napkins in the trash, along with Jordan's. "Right now all I want to do is enjoy this band."

Jordan and I blend into the crowd of Into the Mist

fans right as the band takes the stage. I try to push as far forward as I can, since I'm so short and all I can really see is a bunch of shoulders and heads in front of me. Luckily we find a little pocket I can peek through about a third of the way back from the stage, and we finally relax and enjoy the music.

For me, there's nothing in the world like live music. The energy from the band onstage is electric and contagious, and it pumps out through the speakers, filling me up in places I didn't even know were empty. My ears ring with feedback and instruments and voices, and I feel it across my skin and all the way down to my bones. The music becomes my bones, really. And my blood and my veins and my skin, until I'm completely owned by the music.

It's weird to look around at all these people—people I would probably never hang out with at school—and know that we're all here for the same reason. This music means something to all of us, no matter how different we are. This music brings us all together, makes us all feel alive.

That's the energy now, under this tent. All of us packed in like sardines, with music rolling over us like waves. Jordan and I jump around to the beat and sing out loud with Into the Mist's vocalist, a tall Black girl with the longest legs I've ever seen in my life, as she struts around on the stage in her leather shorts. The rest of the crowd does the same, and I smile even as sweat drips down my face and the dude next to me steps on my foot while he's jumping around and someone spills a drink down my back. I don't even care. I'm living in the music now, and normal rules don't apply.

And it may sound kinda woo-woo, but I can feel my dad here, too. His energy is under this tent with me and Jordan, buzzing between us, in the space between the bass and the vocals, and that energy makes us jump higher and scream louder.

After about forty-five minutes of a set that feels more like a workout, Into the Mist thanks us and walks off the stage, and the crowd under the tent dissipates. Energized and exhausted, Jordan and I walk to the open space outside of the tent to catch our breaths.

"What's next?" he asks once he evens his breathing out a bit.

I pull out my phone. "Well, the Gold Parade starts in an hour, and I'm not missing them. I saw an internet cafe tent over there with laptops set up. I want this phone battery to last as long as possible, so I was thinking about using the computers to do some research on interview questions for the Known, respond to some messages, stuff like that. You want to come?"

Jordan looks at his phone, too, and I can tell from his face that he has a more appealing offer via text.

"Let me guess, what's her name with the hair and the invisible flashlight wants to meet up?"

He grins. "How did you guess?" His voice gets serious. "Is that cool?"

"Does it matter if I say it's not?" I say, rolling my eyes. "I'm fine on my own." Truth be told, the idea of meeting up with Jay for the Gold Parade keeps popping up in the back of my head, and not having Jordan with me will give me some time to sort those feelings out a little bit.

I love Jordan, but it's nice to take a little break from being the responsible one keeping our lives together. When he's gone, I can just worry about myself. And, let's face it, I'm way less drama than he is.

"Go." I push him on the back, then wipe my hands on my shorts because his tank top is totally soaked through with sweat. "But stop by the bathroom to dry off first. You're disgusting."

Jordan promises to text me later, then takes off. I head over to the internet cafe tent I saw earlier, between the Cactus Stage and the Outdoor Stage. I walk through the glass doors, and I'm immediately hit with a blast of air-conditioning that feels amazing on my sticky, sweaty skin.

"Aaah," I say as I walk toward one of the open laptops lining the wall. Most of the crowd packed into this fancy tent are sprawled over the trio of couches in the middle or gathered around the several pillars that litter the room, each lined up and down with electrical outlets for phone charging. Fortunately, I have my phone savior Hipster Matthew and don't need that service.

I turn on the laptop webcam and film a quick live video, explaining the contest and encouraging my handful of viewers to like and share the hashtagged photos on my feed. I decide to test the waters by asking them to reply with what they'd like to see me share from the festival, and I manage to post a couple of pictures by grabbing them from my cloud. I'm tempted to address the "WTF? Jay Bankar? EEEWW" comments that have popped up on the group picture Hipster Matthew made me post, but I purposely ignore that topic for now. I mean, I've been telling myself *WTF? Jay Bankar? EEEWW* all day, and if I can't even explain his confusing presence in my life to myself, I certainly can't make my commenters understand. Why did I keep talking to him after I found out who he was? Why did I smile at him?

Why is meeting him at the Gold Parade the only thing on my mind?

My inbox is full, but none of the messages are urgent, so I search for the Known in an effort to come up with interview questions, just in case I win. They have been interviewed so many times that they've been asked literally everything. I'm able to put a few boring questions into a note on my phone, but I figure that if I'm bored typing them up, the Known will be even more bored answering them, and viewers will be too bored to actually watch. I wish my dad was still around every single day, to watch action movies with late at night when Jordan and Mom have gone to bed, to eat all the drive-thru fries with before we even get the food home, to get new music recommendations, complete with insider information on my new favorite bands. But especially on days like this, when I could ask him for advice on how he did his job, how he interviewed every band and artist you could think of without being so basic.

Finally, I spend the last few minutes before it's time to head over to the Gold Parade researching my scavenger hunt competitors. Apparently, Cody is the girl of the podcasting pair, and the guy, Corey, is her boyfriend. And it turns out Quan is the biggest social media influencer of us all, with a Twitch that has over a million subscribers who tune in to watch him play *Counter-Strike*.

The last thing I do is pull up Jay's channel. I scroll through the still frames from his videos, and I'm reminded that they aren't all pranks and awfulness. There are a few recent ones that have to do with more serious topics: one called "No, I'm Not Muslim, But So What If I Was?" that I remember was actually interesting and thoughtful and not full of fart jokes, as well as one called "Indian People Are South Asian, Actually" that I somehow missed, but I notice these two have far and away the lowest views out of all the other videos, and the comments say things like "Boring!!!!!!!!!!!!!!!" However, he quickly went back to the tried and true with his most recent offering, titled "Smelly Pirate Hooker," which I immediately recognize as a quote from *Anchorman*, one of Jordan's favorites. A quick glance around the charging tent confirms that no one is paying attention to my screen, so I turn the volume on the computer down low and click PLAY.

A generic song plays as "You Know I'm Right," with Jay's stupid, punchable face forming both of the *O*'s, and the dot of the *i*, fills the screen. Then the graphic fades away, and Jay is sitting there in his normal set, some generic room that looks like a storage unit, and he launches into his usual schtick.

"So, there's this chick who works at my local Coffee Coffin," he says, smarming it up into the camera. "She's a Smelly Pirate Hooker." He launches into a story about how he tried to hit on her and she ignored him. I mean, who can blame her, especially if she's trying to work? The more he talks about what an ugly bitch this girl is, which is rich, considering he's the one who hit on her in the first place, the more I am filled with rage. Why did I agree to meet up with this douche? Odds are, I'm going to be the next Smelly Pirate Hooker, the unwitting star of his next video, mocked and ridiculed for daring to turn him down.

"We're going to get back at her today for dissing me," he says.

I'm about to turn it off, because I really don't need to see him harassing this innocent girl at her place of work, but then I see it. His videos are always so slickly produced, with perfect cuts and editing. But here is a bad cut. It happens so quickly that a normal person who wasn't analyzing every second of this video probably wouldn't notice at all, but I catch it, and it shows so much. Jay is done talking, and in a second before the video cuts to him outside the Coffee Coffin, his face falls. Changes. Morphs into something else. The hard, unfriendly expression he keeps in front of the camera, the one I saw briefly when signing up for the scavenger hunt, falls away, and for a split second, I see him, the Jay I met last night. It's like he wears a mask when he's filming, and when he thinks the camera isn't running, it slips right off.

And it's in that quick moment I second-guess my decision. There *is* something more going on with Jay Bankar, and I want him to explain himself. I deserve that explanation. This poor girl from the Coffee Coffin deserves it, too.

I close the video and check the time. Fifteen minutes to get myself over to the Gold Parade's set.

Fifteen minutes to figure out if I'm going to give Jay Bankar a second chance.

As I cross the grounds, I shoot a text to Jordan asking how everything is going, and I wait for an answer. After five minutes with no reply, I slide my phone into my back pocket. I thought I wanted space to figure this out for myself, but, let's be real, it would have been nice to have him dole out that older and wiser brotherly advice. Apparently, I'll be making this decision on my own.

A pretty solid crowd has already gathered for the Gold Parade under the tent at the Cactus Stage. The sun is lowering in the sky, and it's cooling off a little bit. The paradox of the desert. It's blazing hot during the day, but it chills down considerably after sunset. I'll probably have to go back to camp after this to grab a hoodie and change into jeans.

I briefly consider going now. Running back to the campsite, skipping the Gold Parade altogether, changing into my warm clothes, and then having fun for the rest of the night. Watching bands, eating Spice Pie, maybe interviewing some festivalgoers, either on my own or with Jordan if he ever decides to show up.

But, of course, I know exactly what I'm doing. I'm trying to get out of making this choice about Jay, to decide by not deciding, and I hate when I do that because I always end up unhappy, like when I didn't want to pick between sitting next to Jordan or my elementary school bestie, Ashanti, on a bus trip in third grade, and I ended up stuck next to Mrs. Sanderson because both of them gave up on me and sat with other friends.

Ugh, what do I do? I could seek Jay out and talk to him, putting myself out there, even though the odds are pretty high that he could be playing me. Or I could purposely keep my distance. But will I be able to go home on Sunday knowing I never found out what was behind Jay Bankar?

Everything in my brain tells me to stay as far away as possible. But there's some other part of me that wants to seek him out. It's not even the part of me that wants to hear what he has to say. It's the part of me that keeps playing that smile of his on repeat in my head. His laugh. His arms. That one second of his real face I saw in his video. The part of me I have been trying to silence since this morning but for the life of me can't manage to shut up.

That part of me feels like such a traitor. Because as much as I know intellectually that Jay Bankar is the actual worst, I simply can't manage to hold all that tightly to my hatred of him. Every time I've been around him, he's been so different from my expectations, and, if I'm totally honest with myself, he's never once been that guy from his videos. It's a damn mystery.

If he's going to be able to give me a reason to not hate him like my brain tells me I should, I guess I can try to give it a listen.

Scanning everyone as I go, I walk around the back of the crowd of fans. Jay's tall, but not so tall that I expect to see his head popping out above everyone else's. It seems like all the people in this crowd have black hair all of a sudden, and the shadows of dusk are making everyone's skin tone look the same.

Now I really wish I had Jordan. He got all of the height in our twinship, and that would sure be useful in spotting a needle in a huge haystack of dudes.

The Gold Parade walks onstage, and a loud whoop erupts from the crowd. The band hits the first notes of the opening song on their latest album, and, in an instant, the mood in the tent changes. That's all it takes to get the previously mellow crowd energized and moving.

And just like that, as if the music is pointing me in the right direction, Jay enters my line of vision. He's jumping around and singing along, and there isn't a trace of the online asshole on his face at all. He's happy and free and in love with the music. He looks exactly the way I feel.

I let myself watch him for a few seconds, enjoying his smile and the way he shouts the chorus of the song along with the band, and the way his tank top gets pulled up a little bit when he pumps his arm in the air, showing off a dark, flat stomach that the traitor part of me wants to see more of. Then I tell myself I'm doing it. I'm going to go enjoy this band with him and then I'll listen to whatever he was trying to say to me earlier after the scavenger hunt. I'll keep an open mind. It's not a second chance; it's just . . . a chance.

The opening song draws to a close, and I push my

way through the pumped-up crowd. I'm only a little bit away from Jay now, close enough to yell out his name if I want to and have him hear me, when I see the last thing I expected to see. A manicured hand rests itself on his arm and squeezes playfully.

I follow the hand up its tan arm, and I don't even have to make it to the perfectly made-up face and impeccably balayaged hair to know that Jay is watching the Gold Parade with Sadie Díaz.

CHAPTER 6

>>> • <<<

SADIE LAUGHS AND JAY LAUGHS AND SHE SQUEEZES again and then elbows him lightly in the side. And before I figure out what to do, the band starts their second song and the singing and jumping and crowd-pulsing begins again. I'm not caught up in it this time, though. I'm apart from it. Alone.

What the hell is going on in my head? Only a few hours ago, I hated Jay Bankar with every fiber of my being. And, really, we only spent an hour or so together having fun. We flirted, sure, and took one selfie together, but that doesn't mean anything.

There is no logical reason to feel disappointed to see him with another girl. I should be relieved. He wants to hang out with Sadie. Of course he does. Why wouldn't he? She's beautiful and nice. Hell, *I* want to hang out with her.

It must be the universe telling me I was right about Jay Bankar. My instincts telling me to be cautious and stay away and not trust him were exactly on point. *Jay Bankar is no good. Keep your distance.*

And when the universe talks, I listen.

Even when I was really, really hoping it was going to be wrong this time.

I don't want Jay Bankar to ruin this show for me. I love the Gold Parade too much to let the experience be tainted by his bad vibes. But I stay where I am, away from him and away from Sadie, and I enjoy myself alone. I take pictures and I dance and I shoot a quick video and I sing at the top of my lungs. But my live music experience is missing something this time. A little bit of the energy is gone, and I miss it.

Almost an hour later, the band thanks everyone by saying, "We're the Gold Parade from Pasadena," which causes me to scream without even realizing I'm doing it. Something about hearing my hometown called out like that triggers a Pavlovian woo-girl response.

And somehow, in this crowded, loud tent, Jay must hear me. Because he turns around at that instant, scanning the crowd. My first instinct is to hide behind the gigantic dude to my left. But then, no. I want Jay to see me. To see I was here and I was close enough to see him and I chose not to seek him out. So when his eyes find mine in the crowd, I look right back with hard, unbreaking eye contact, keep my face totally neutral, and shrug. Then I turn as quickly as I can manage with crowds of people filing out of the tent on either side of me, and I join in the stream of humanity and file out myself, leaving him watching me and, given that expression on his face, wondering what happened.

I sneak myself behind a huge sculpture of a heart with a giant arrow piercing it, and I pull out my phone. Still no reply from Jordan, so I text him again. The really awesome bands are starting at the Main Stage and the Outdoor Stage in about forty-five minutes, so it's the perfect time to slip into something warmer and come back out on the grass for a night full of amazing music.

And that's exactly what I do. My brother never replies to any of my texts, which has me a mixture of sad and worried and annoyed. Tomorrow is our Bad Day, so he better be getting this out of his system today so we can get through tomorrow together. Jay never shows up in the corner of my eye or in the line for S'mores on a Stick or in the crowd waiting for the bathroom, which leaves me feeling both a lot relieved and a little disappointed.

I finally accept the fact that I'm on my own for the rest of the night, and I follow the crowd over to the Outdoor Stage to catch Boldface Republic.

"Andi!"

For a second my heart squeezes, hoping it will be Jay. But as I turn around, I see Quan, the gamer from the scavenger hunt, emerging from the crowd behind me and holding hands with a short white guy with perfect blond hair and an even more perfect smile.

"Hey, Quan," I say, waving. "You heading to Boldface Republic?"

"Yeah, I guess," he says, rolling his eyes. "They're not really my scene, but this guy loves them, so what can you do?" He lifts up the hand that's attached to the blond guy. "This is my boyfriend, Dan. Babe, this is Andi. She won the first round of that scavenger hunt thing you made me sign up for."

"I'm obsessed with the Known," Dan says in a tone I can only describe as gushing. "If there is even the tiniest possibility of me getting to breathe the same air as Bernard White, I'm going to make him take it."

"See?" Quan says, shrugging. "Compromises."

I fall into step with them as we continue making our way toward the Outdoor Stage's crowd. "Why didn't you come do the scavenger hunt with Quan, then? He could have used the help."

"Hey!" Quan says in mock outrage. "I got stuck trying to find a celebrity. I gave up and had to do a completely different line on the card. It took forever."

I'm about to mention Lukas MacDonald, but Dan jumps in to explain his absence. "I'm also obsessed with Still Standing at the End of the World. There was no way I was missing their set. They played three brand-new songs!"

"The things I do for this one, I swear." Quan rolls his eyes, but his voice is playful. "So, where's your brother?"

"Ah, he ditched me." I try to keep my words light, matching Quan's playful tone.

"What?" Dan says. "That sucks. Have you been alone all day?"

I shrug. "No, not all day. It's fine. I mean, it's not fine, but it's kind of his thing, so I'm used to it."

"Well, hang out with us for this set," Quan says, waving toward the stage.

Having these guys invite me to hang out with them is such a relief, especially after the double rejection of my brother and Jay. Sure, I feel a bit like a third wheel, but it's only for one band.

We find a clear spot with a mostly unobstructed view and get comfortable as we wait for the band to take the stage. "So, what got you to sign up for the scavenger hunt?" Quan asks. "Are you obsessed with Bernard White, too?"

"Not exactly. Although my mom is."

Dan makes a face.

I explain it all to Quan, word-vomiting out everything about Jordan's SCU scholarship, our dad and what happened to him, and our financial situation. I'm sure it's TMI, but I've been hanging out by myself for so long that I can't make myself stop talking now that I have an audience.

"Well, not sure if this is good or bad news, but I'm going to SCU next year," Dan says with a smile. "Hopefully it ends up being good news, but if not, maybe I can sneak you along in my backpack."

"You are? No way!" I turn to Quan, "I thought Matthew said you were from San Francisco?"

"I am," Quan says. "And so is he."

"I'm wrapping up at City College of San Francisco this semester, and I'm moving to LA in a few months. He doesn't even want to talk to me about it. He's in denial."

"Why don't you move to LA, too?"

"I go to San Francisco State. I don't graduate until next year."

"So you did community college before transferring to SCU?" I've always known community college is an option, but it always gave me thirteenth-grade vibes.

"Hell, yeah," Dan says. "I saved myself, like, a hundred fifty thousand dollars. SCU tuition is no joke."

"Tell me about it," I say. "If my brother didn't play basketball, he'd be screwed. Too bad they don't have a crafting team." I have some questions for Dan, but the members of Boldface Republic announce their arrival on the stage with a few hits on the drums and some random guitar strums before they launch into their first song, and our conversation is over. We're flooded with lights and sound and music that moves us to dance and sing and forget about everything else for a while.

An hour later, after the band wraps up their set, all three of us are sweaty, and Quan and Dan definitely look as exhausted as I feel. This long day catches up to me in a rush of heavy eyelids and cloudy thoughts, and even though the night-one headliners are taking the Main Stage soon, I want nothing more than to be curled into the comfort of my sleeping bag.

"I think I'm calling it a night," I say, twisting my sweaty hair up into a topknot. "Are you guys heading back to the campsite?"

"I think we're going to check out the Main Stage before we leave." Quan's shirt is drenched, and he grabs the front of it with two fingers and pulls it away from his skin as we make our way across the grounds. "And, no. We got a hotel room in town."

Dan's perfectly styled hair has flopped into a sweaty mess on his forehead. "I don't camp."

"Neither do I," says Quan. "I need a bed. And a shower."

"Hey," I say, feeling the need to defend our cozy little campsite. "We have a shower. You just have to wait in a line and wear flip-flops and go in there with, like, ten other people."

Quan barks out a laugh. "Yeah, no. That's not happening."

The festival entrance looms ahead of me, so I say good night to Quan and Dan with promises to see Quan tomorrow for more scavenger hunt fun.

"Bye, Andi," Dan says, waving. "Hopefully I'll see you at SCU next year."

"Well, you'll definitely see my brother. Maybe you can keep him in line for me if I don't get this scavenger hunt locked in."

Dan raises his hand for a high five. "Tell him to look for me."

"Stay safe, Andi," Quan says, and we wave goodbye.

The crowd is thick as I walk through the festival gates, and I make my way back to the campsite with everyone else who decided it was time to call it a night or at least relocate the party. I wish I hadn't had to say good night to Quan and Dan, because suddenly walking back to camp alone seems more than a little overwhelming.

A group of about five girls in their twenties are walking ahead of me, and I hurry to catch up to them. "Excuse me!" I call, and they all stop to turn around. "Hi. I can't find my brother, and I'm not wild about walking back to the campsite alone in the dark. Do you mind if I tag along with you?" I'm okay doing things alone—this is hardly the first time Jordan has ditched me. But I'm not stupid, and I know there is safety in numbers.

The girls exchange glances, obviously trying to decide if this is some kind of trick, but then they nod. One of them says, "Sure," and they turn around and keep walking to the campground, ignoring me as they finish their enthusiastic debrief about the day. There was some drama between one of the girls and her ex, who showed up to the festival with some girl they all work with at Chili's, and they are going through an extensive play-by-play of everyone's words, actions, and thoughts all day long to figure out who is at fault.

Usually, listening in on other people's stories is my jam. But now that I'm alone and don't have music and crowds of people and the hubbub of the festival to distract me, I'm left alone with my thoughts. I watch every person we pass, looking for my brother. And for Jay.

Jay's voice carries through the air before I see him. It sounds like he's on the other side of my new group of friends, on the trail back to the campsite, so I scoot over as far from him as I can get in an attempt to hide. These girls are all pretty tall, and I am almost certain I'm blocked from his view by the one who got screwed over by her ex.

The girls talk so loudly that it's difficult to hear exactly what Jay says. Since I feel sufficiently hidden, I allow myself to turn slightly so I can see who he's talking to.

Ah, his brother. Of course. No wonder Jay's voice is so loud. Now that I see the waving hands and hostile body language, it's obvious they're arguing.

I listen as carefully as I can, but the ex-boyfriend story has taken a particularly dramatic turn, with the ex apparently posting some pictures on his story that I really wish I could see, and the girls' voices increase in volume and pitch, so the conversation between Jay and his brother is nearly inaudible. I do hear "scavenger hunt" and "festival" and "winning" and "Matthew" and "I hate that" and "Sadie."

Then Jay says something that has me shook.

". . . ruined things with Andi . . ."

What? Why is he talking about me?

Well, now what? Do I sneak closer to hear more and risk getting spotted?

Before I get to make a decision, though, one of the girls in my adopted group stops in her tracks. "Our tent is up here," she says, pointing at the first street of campsites past the bathroom area. "Are you going to be okay?"

"What? Oh, yeah. Thanks for letting me walk with you." I smile at them as they break away from me, turning down the street to their campsite and leaving me to fend for myself on the last few streets. Well, I'm not completely alone. Jay and his brother are right behind me, and there's nothing left to keep them from seeing me now, since we're all heading to the same destination.

I try to walk on along, as unassuming as possible, doing everything but breaking into a casual whistle, but that only lasts a second before I'm spotted.

"Oh, look who it is," Jay's brother says, his voice venomous.

"Dev," Jay says. "Stop it."

"Oh, sorry," he replies. "I would hate to be rude." His

voice is so sarcastic, but I have no idea what he's giving me or Jay shit about. I've hardly talked to this guy. I wonder if he found out Jay told me about Lukas MacDonald, but I doubt Jay would willingly divulge that information.

"I'm just trying to walk back to my tent and go to sleep. Please leave me out of whatever family drama you two have going on." I quicken my pace, hoping to put as much distance between myself and the Bankar brothers as I can, but these short legs of mine don't get me as far as I want.

"Andi, wait!" It's Jay, and he trots up until we fall into step. From behind us, his brother groans in frustration.

"What do you want?" I swear, every time I thought I was wrong about this guy in the past twenty-four hours, something happened to prove to me that I shouldn't second-guess myself.

"My brother is a dick. I'm sorry."

I take a good look at Jay for the first time tonight. Like me, he threw on a hoodie, and he's wearing the Dodgers hat that made him unrecognizable to me the night before. I wish he hadn't covered up those glorious arms. They would give me something fabulous to focus on right now, and I could really use it.

I shrug. "I'm not going to say it's okay, because it's not, but I appreciate your apology."

"Fair enough," Jay says, shoving his hands deep into the pockets of his hoodie.

"You don't have to walk with me, you know."

"I know, but it's dark and you're alone. People are creeps."

"People like you?"

"People like Dev."

"What's his deal, anyway?"

He turns around to look at his brother, then shakes his head slightly. "I was going to tell you all about it at the Gold Parade, but you didn't show up." He's trying to sound nonchalant, but his voice reveals that he's bummed. "I get it."

"Well, I did show up." Now it's my turn to shove my hands into my hoodie pockets. "But you were a little occupied. I didn't want to intrude."

He cocks his head.

"You found someone else to enjoy the show with," I say. "Nothing wrong with that. I'm glad Sadie made it to the Gold Parade. Did she like them? It looked like you were having a pretty good time with her."

"Oh God," Jay says. "Andi. Sadie was just there. Because *you* told her to check them out. And she was alone. I really wanted to—"

"You don't have to explain," I say. Then my voice gets soft. "I just wanted to let you know I did show up. And I found you. But I didn't want to interrupt." As soon as the words are out of my mouth, it feels like I gave something huge about myself away. I wish I could pull it all back in and hide that confession away, especially after Jay's face softens. Instead, I change the subject as quickly as possible by talking as much as I can and not letting him get a word in. "The set was awesome, though, right? They were so great. I loved that they played some of the stuff from their first album. I feel like they hardly play that old stuff anymore. Who else did you see today?" I launch into a list of all the bands I saw in the evening, including Boldface Republic with Quan and Dan, and by the time I'm done with my list and mini reviews of each set, we're back at our tents.

Dev doesn't say anything to us and huffs grumpily over to their campsite, disappearing into their tent but making lots of angry noises from the inside.

"Does he always act like a child?"

"Pretty much," Jay says. "He's four years older than me. He's almost twenty-two. But you would never know it from the way he throws a tantrum."

"He's a total baby."

Jay nods. "He has a one-track mind. The channel is his pride and joy, and he gets grumpy when we're not actively working on it. He's a workaholic, so he doesn't understand that I just want to relax and have fun this weekend."

"Well." I take my hands out of my hoodie pockets and

shove them into my back pockets. "That was cool of you to walk with me. I appreciate it. But I've had a long day, and I should probably get some rest."

"Where's your brother?" he asks.

I pull out my phone to see if there has been any word from Jordan, but tumbleweeds are rolling through my text inbox. I shrug.

"Did he seriously ditch you again?"

"He's not usually like this," I say, even though he is. "It's just . . ." I trail off. I don't really want to get into my brother and my dad with Jay. Even though I can't figure him out at all, it doesn't mean he can be trusted. "It's a weird time right now."

"Well, I think it sucks that he's leaving you all alone at night like this."

"Why do you care?" I don't mean for it to come out sounding so snippy, but I guess I can't help it when it comes to Jay Bankar. I seem to have two modes with this guy. Major Bitch or Trying Not to Flirt Obviously.

And sometimes I downshift from one right into the other.

"Because I care about your safety. Is that okay?"

It doesn't escape my notice that Jay's voice has taken on a tenderness during this admission of his and also that he has scooted closer. It's a microscopic closeness, but it's there. He's closer.

"I can tell you can take care of yourself," he says, and

he lets out a sharp laugh. "There's no doubt about that. But other people suck, and it's never a good idea to be alone at things like this. That's all."

"Okay." His genuine concern shocks me. It's something else I'm putting in my WTF IRL Jay column. Because there's no way the Jay from his videos would be this concerned about another human being, much less a girl.

"Who *are* you?" I ask.

"What do you mean?"

I find that this time I have scooted forward a microscopic amount. Now I'm closer and I'm searching his face for the thing that's going to help unlock the mystery of this guy. A mystery I really do want to solve. "Why are you so nice to me?"

"This is who I am," he says, his voice almost a whisper. "That's not me. On the videos."

I shake my head. "Nuh-uh. I need more of an explanation than that. Because I've seen many of your videos—"

"And I thought you weren't a fan," he says, letting out a soft laugh.

"I hate-watch them. Your disgusting opinions fuel my feminist rage."

He shakes his head. "You have to believe me when I say that's not who I am."

"So are you going to tell me what that means now?"

He looks back at his campsite, where his brother is

lurking behind the tent. He's probably watching us like a big creeper.

"I can't right now. Tomorrow? Can we meet up for real?"

"Well, we have a standing date with Hipster Matthew."

Jay smiles. "That guy is the best. I can't figure out if the Crocs are supposed to be ironic or not."

A loud commotion comes from Jay's tent area—it honestly sounds like Dev is bowling with their lantern—and I assume that's Jay's cue from his brother-slash-keeper that it's time to stop consorting with the enemy.

"Well, he'll be there tomorrow," he says, jerking his head toward his tent. "But hopefully I can ditch him and we can hang out?"

"And you'll tell me what's up with him?"

"It's . . . complicated. But you haven't answered me yet, so I'm asking for the third time now. Andi, will you please hang out with me tomorrow?"

And despite my brain, again, flashing sirens and red lights, unrolling caution tape, and yelling at me to get the hell out, I find myself saying, "Fine, Jay Bankar. We can hang out tomorrow. But you have to promise to divulge your secrets to me."

"I'll tell you everything. Promise," he says, offering his pinkie to me. I wrap my pinkie around his and squeeze, and we both smile at each other. "Okay, I have to go."

"Yeah," I say. "I should go to bed. Right after I leave my brother some more angry messages."

"I can leave some for you, if you want. I can think of plenty of things to say to that guy right now."

"No need. My words will have enough sting."

And the whole time we say this, we haven't dropped our pinkie promise. We're still standing there, pinkie fingers entwined, smiling like maniacs.

"Well," I say. "Thanks for walking me back here. Even though I was a bitch to you."

"Thanks for letting me. Even though you hate me and I was cheating on you with Sadie."

I shake my head. "Of all the people."

"But you hung out with Quan tonight, so . . ."

"Quan and his *boyfriend*."

"Two dudes. That's even worse, Andi."

He finally breaks the pinkie promise and pulls me forward into a hug. I can't remember anyone but my mom who has ever initiated a hug with me, because I always get to them first. "I can't believe you would think for a second I would ditch you for her," he says into my hair, and my body lights up like a firework.

I smile into the darkness before I pull away. "Your brother is probably going to burn that tent down if you don't go now."

"You're right. Good night, Andi. See you tomorrow."

"Good night, Jay." I give a little wave, and I crawl into my tent.

Once inside, away from his face, I stretch out on my

air mattress and wonder what I have just done. Not only did I flirt with Jay Bankar again, this time with full knowledge of who he is, I also agreed to meet up with him tomorrow. And I hugged him! God, what's wrong with me? Jordan leaves me alone and takes my rational decision-making abilities with him. Maybe he's the one who needs to be babysitting me.

There's something about Jay Bankar that keeps me all full of confusing, conflicting emotions. Extreme hatred and now this. The feeling that all concept of right and wrong, good and bad flew out the window with one flash of that killer smile of his.

He's dangerous.

But I kind of like it.

Okay, I really like it.

Which is also dangerous.

My sleeping bag cocoons around me as I text Mom good night, then try Jordan one more time. No reply to my text, and his phone goes straight to voice mail. I leave a message anyway.

"Jordan, I am both worried and pissed. I'm trying to give you a pass because I know what tomorrow is, but it's hard to muster up sympathy when I'm alone in this tent in the dark and surrounded by strangers on all sides. Please call or text me back whenever you get this, even if it's in the middle of the night. And you best be by my side tomorrow because you know I need you." I play up my anger in hopes of getting some kind of reply from him, but, let's be real, I know nothing is coming.

Is this how it's going to be next year at SCU? Jordan does this stuff all the time, but it's not going to fly when he has basketball and school to stay on top of. Although I guess I'm not doing a very good job of keeping an eye on him when I don't have any idea where he is and he won't answer my calls. But it's got to be easier on SCU's small campus.

As I wait for a reply from Jordan that I know won't come, I search for Jay's photo stream and start scrolling through it. There are a lot of stills from his videos, but also shots of him laughing at the beach, him eating a bunch of yummy-looking Indian food, and him at lots and lots of concerts. I'm way, way back on his feed when a particularly aggressive swipe up turns into a double tap on a photo of Jay holding a dachshund puppy. I drop my phone like it's on fire when I realize that I have accidentally liked one of his pictures from two whole years ago. I scramble to find my phone in the dark, and it takes what feels like three hours, but I'm able to un-like the photo. Adrenaline pumps through my body like I just parachuted off an airplane. *He's asleep. There's no way he saw that. Nothing to worry about.*

But not even ten seconds later, a notification pops up. From Jay Bankar. In my DMs. Oh my God.

JAYBANKAR: 👀 I see you digging deep in my pics

ANDIKENNEDYCRAFTS: Just doing research on the competition

JAYBANKAR: Right

I thought you were going to bed

ANDIKENNEDYCRAFTS: I was. Just trying to wait up for Jordan

I thought *you* were going to bed

JAYBANKAR: I was. Just checking out the competition

ANDIKENNEDYCRAFTS: ??

JAYBANKAR: Hand lettering looks so . . . complicated. How long did that take to learn?

ANDIKENNEDYCRAFTS: You're watching my videos?!?!?

JAYBANKAR: I'm learning a lot, actually

I'm definitely trying to tie-dye a shirt when I get home

ANDIKENNEDYCRAFTS: I can't believe you're up on a Friday night watching crafting videos

JAYBANKAR: I'm watching you do crafting videos

It's a subtle distinction.

ANDIKENNEDYCRAFTS: Well, I'm glad I could entertain you

JAYBANKAR: You are very entertaining

You're obviously passionate about what you do

I like it

ANDIKENNEDYCRAFTS: Well, thanks

JAYBANKAR: Ok, going to bed for real now

Feel free to keep creeping on my pics

I don't mind

ANDIKENNEDYCRAFTS: Don't flatter yourself

JAYBANKAR: Sweet dreams, Andi

See you tomorrow

CHAPTER 7

>>> • <<<

THE NEXT MORNING, SATURDAY, I'M WOKEN UP MUCH earlier than I want to be. According to the calendar, it's the worst day of the year, the anniversary of our dad's death. And already it looks like it's going to be another bad one.

I only put in one earplug before dozing off so I could hear my phone if Jordan called or texted me. And the white boys next door decided to throw us for a loop and start in with a lesser-known '90s pop queens appreciation party at somewhere around four a.m.

Also, at some point in the middle of the night, my air mattress deflated, so I spent half the night rolling around with only a few layers of too-thin sleeping bag, plastic, and vinyl between my back and the rocks and gravel on the ground.

Oh, and Jordan is here. He stumbled in sometime after I went to sleep, clomped around a bit, and then passed out on his sleeping bag. His clomping likely has something to do with my flat air mattress. And it definitely has something to do with the fact that I can't stop scratching my arm. He must have left the door to the tent unzipped a crack, because some unknown bug appears to have feasted upon my body.

Here we go again. Yeah, this festival is fun, and I want to somehow film a video that will turn my channel into a pile of money, but escaping the Anniversary Day Curse was also part of the plan, for both me and Jordan. We've both finally gotten to the point where our grief isn't a constant thing. When it first happened, it was like a never-ending migraine. The pain over losing Dad was ceaseless; it kept us from performing even the most basic of tasks, and the only way to get through it was to sit alone in a dark room. As the years have gone on, the migraine has dulled—it's no longer constant, and it pops up less and less. It's always there, though, like something pulsating, dull and throbbing, in the very back of my head. Jordan and I both fully bought into the fantasy of getting out of LA and leaving the curse, and the aching grief that's all tangled up with it, behind in traffic as we sped down the freeway into the desert.

But as soon as I wake up at this ungodly hour with my brother stinking of booze and snoring obnoxiously, my arms covered in red bumps, and jagged stones digging into my back, I wonder why we didn't examine the flaws in that shoddy plan a little more. I guess when you're desperate to feel anything, you'll go along with whatever ridiculous plan comes your way.

I manage to get some half-assed sleep until the sun comes out, and then I give up and head to the bathroom, eager for the opportunity to stretch my legs. Next to the bathrooms, the line for the shower curls only halfway around the building, considerably shorter than yesterday's, and I run back to the tent to get my shower stuff. A short shower line is an unexpected perk of being up so early, so I hop in behind people who probably never even went to sleep the night before and get myself clean.

The water washes away some of my morning funk, so I'm feeling a small shred of optimism when I head back to our tent. Maybe the Anniversary Day Curse had its way with me early and will leave me alone to enjoy the rest of my day.

But then I run into Dev Bankar.

If the world was kind, there would be somewhere for me to hide from him. But the world is a brutal hellscape, so, of course, Dev and I are the only people walking on our lonely campsite street. Since the damp beach towel I'm wrapped in doesn't have any magical powers, I just throw back my shoulders, hold up my chin, and strut by him while simultaneously willing him not to talk to me.

The strutting totally works. The willing, not so much.

"What are you so smug about?" he grumbles as I pass by.

I stop, the hand not holding my shower stuff on my hip, and ask, "Excuse me? Have we even met?"

"Don't act like you don't know who I am." He pulls a cigarette out of his pocket and lights it. Ugh. Of course this guy smokes. I'm not even surprised. Awful people have awful habits.

"Oh, I know exactly who you are. I'm just curious why you're speaking to me like you know me when you haven't bothered to introduce yourself or say hello to me at all."

He makes a snorty sound and rolls his eyes. "Whatever," he says. "Will you do me a favor—"

"Doubtful."

"And stay away from my brother?"

Now it's my turn to make a snorty sound. "Me stay away from your brother? God, I've been trying to. I would love to stay away from your brother. Tell him to stay away from me." I start to walk back to my tent, but then I stop and turn around. "You know what? No. Don't tell your brother that. Your brother, despite all my expectations, has been nothing but nice to me. You, on the other hand, have been a raging asshole. So how about you do me a favor and stay away from me, okay? Thanks."

Dev Bankar's mouth hangs slightly open as he watches me whirl around, whipping my wet hair behind me for a dramatic *screw you*, and stomp back to my tent. I'm feeling quite triumphant, wondering if he's ever had a girl tell him off like that, until he lobs another one back at me.

"I checked out your so-called channel yesterday." He lets out a completely humorless laugh. "Pretty pathetic content you have there. Do people outside of your family actually give a shit about that low-budget piece of crap?"

He's trying to bait you, Andi. He's trying to get a rise out of you. I take a deep breath and then another one, but I can't keep it inside. "It's better than being a misogynistic asshole piece of clickbait trash who—"

He laughs, which pisses me off too much to even continue.

"What?"

"And I thought you liked my brother."

Ugh. This jerk-off is seriously pushing my buttons. Insulting my channel. Poking right at my complicated feelings for Jay. I need to get myself out of here before he somehow figures out I have a dead dad and money problems.

"I know what you're doing," I say. "And you're not even worth it. Have a nice day, Dev. I look forward to kicking your ass at today's scavenger hunt like I did yesterday."

He probably says something else, but I do my best to drown it all out by humming the Gold Parade to myself until I get back to the tent. I don't bother staying quiet for my brother. I throw my bathroom stuff back down with all my force and slam my things around, trying to get some of the aggression I'm feeling for Dev out of my system.

I wish I could figure out why this encounter has me so pissed. I mean, I've been expecting this since the moment I realized Jay was Jay Bankar. This rudeness and manipulation and all-around smarmy jerk behavior is hardly a surprise; I just expected it from Jay, not from Dev. But no matter which Bankar brother it's coming from, it's exactly on-brand. It shouldn't have me literally throwing my shampoo bottle across my tent.

"What the hell are you doing?" Jordan mumbles from the corner of our tent. "Stop making noise."

"Oh, sorry," I say, making no attempt to keep my voice down. "Am I disturbing you?"

He covers his head with his pillow. "Not now, okay? Later."

"Oh, sure." I pull on my yoga shorts and a tank top. "Let me worry about your feelings. And Jay's feelings. And his freaking brother's feelings. But go ahead and shit all over me. I don't care."

Jordan grumbles, and I recognize I'm being ridiculous and need to leave. This morning yoga couldn't come at a better time.

But when I get over there, I realize it actually did come at a better time. Some other time. Because there is no morning yoga class going on like there was the morning before.

I pull up the festival app on my phone and see that yoga class is two hours later today. Fabulous. On the one day I really need it. I throw down my mat anyway and do a few sun salutations, then lower myself into child's pose and take some breaths, trying to clear my mind of all the stress that's accumulated before the day has even started.

Then I lay myself back in corpse pose, breathe some more, and talk to my dad.

"Dad," I say softly. "I miss you. I miss you and Jordan misses you and Mom misses you. We are doing okay, but we haven't been the same. Jordan tries to sing songs to the dogs in the neighborhood, but they're never as good as yours. And Mom has never mastered Nana's spaghetti sauce like you did. And I'm trying so hard to go to SCU and be like you, and I don't know if it's going to happen. I don't want to disappoint you, but I don't know if it's going to work out. I'm trying, though. Will you be mad at me if I can't do it?" I'm quiet for a few minutes, and then I say, "I don't want your day to be a stressful one, Dad. Why is it always so bad? Is it you or is it us? If it's you, can you give us a break this year? If it's us, can you show us what we're doing wrong? Your day is sad enough as it is without all of this extra drama."

I stay in savasana for a few more minutes before I tell Dad I love him, stretch out my arms and legs as far as they will go, and stand up to shake out my mat and head back to the tent. I'm feeling better now. More relaxed. I might even be able to go back to sleep if I can get that air mattress inflated again.

Thanks to my earplugs and my yoga mat under my re-inflated air mattress, I do manage to get a little nap in, if you can call going back to sleep at nine o'clock a nap, and I feel a bit like a new person when I wake back up. Maybe Dad is giving me a rare second chance on this day. Maybe I won't have to follow this curse around after all.

Jordan's snoring practically shakes the tent, so I hop out and start cooking breakfast. I call Mom and talk to her as I scramble the Egg Beaters, and the sound of her voice eases the ache in my chest just a little bit. Eventually, the scent of bacon wakes up my sleeping brother—bacon is his siren song—and he stumbles out of the tent, plopping into the folding chair set up next to the camp stove.

"I'm sorry about last night," he says quietly. He's just wearing basketball shorts, his normal sleeping attire, and he scratches absently at his bare chest. "I guess I got an early start on today. Drowning my sorrows and whatnot. Ugh, I don't know why this is so hard."

"It's hard because we lost our *dad*, Jordan."

"I know. I just needed to forget about everything for a little while."

I stare at him for as long as I can look away from the bacon without burning it, and then I get back to cooking. "I was seriously worried about you."

"My battery died. You have the backup chargers. And you knew I was fine."

"No. I didn't know that. There are thousands of people here. Statistically, some percentage of them have to be legit murderers. I had no idea who you were with, and you wouldn't answer any of my calls or texts. I know you're going through your crap, but so am I. At least check in."

"It's early, Andi. Please don't yell. And I apologized, okay? I messed up. I'm sorry. It won't happen again."

"Just not today, okay? I need you."

"I know you do. And I need you, too." He leans over in his chair and wraps his long arms around my waist.

"Is this supposed to be a hug?"

"Yes. And it's a good hug."

"It is a good hug. But you can let me go now."

He lets out a grunt and drops his arms, leaning back into the folding chair. "Now that we have that worked out, can you please hook me up with some of that bacon? I'm dying over here."

We eat our food in silence. Well, silence aside from our neighbors' awful trap music that is practically shaking our tent. Dad hovers between us, though.

"I've had a bad day so far," I say finally.

Jordan raises his eyebrow.

I fill him in on my morning. Bad sleep, no yoga, "and a charming run-in with the older, nastier Bankar brother."

"What?"

"Oh, Dev tried to intimidate me by being an asshole

and talking crap on my videos and telling me to stay away from his brother and all this other dumb shit."

"Why would you need to stay away from his brother?"

I fill him in on last night's Bankar encounter. "Although you would know this if you hadn't ditched me. Where were you, anyway?"

He takes a sip of iced coffee and stares at the tent next to us. "Just with Monica from school and her older sister and her friends."

"And you were drinking?"

"Yeah. But that's it. Don't worry. I was only . . . preparing for today, I guess."

He doesn't need to explain himself further, because I feel this deep down in my bones. The years keep moving on, the grief getting incrementally easier to manage, but this day never gets easier. Daily life has become less of a struggle—every single waking moment is no longer filled with memories of Dad, even though he's always there in some way, his presence floating just under the surface of everything I do. The actual day, though? It's always hard, always bad. Jordan and I keep trying to find different ways to deal with the pain, the loss—going away for the weekend, exercise, alcohol, straight-up denial. But from the look on my brother's face—and I'm sure the look on mine, if it matches how I feel inside—none of those things work.

You can't hide from grief, and you can't drown it or

trick it or mask it. It always finds you because it becomes part of your DNA.

"Well," I say, gathering up our breakfast trash, "we need to try to have a good day today. Try to turn it around."

Jordan smiles. "Yeah. I don't think Dad would want us always having such a bad day every year. Especially at Cabazon."

"I talked to him this morning."

"You did?"

"Yeah. Since there was no yoga when I thought there was, I did my savasana and then told him we missed him and asked him if he could ease up on the drama for this year. We'll see if he listens."

"Dad did always love the drama."

Once we're all cleaned up and dressed and set for the day, we only have a couple of hours before it's time for scavenger hunt task number two with Hipster Matthew and our #MobilocityFamily. Jordan and I roam around the campground, which has a general store full of ridiculously overpriced food and goods, more phone charging stations, and a few stands and food trucks selling treats and snacks. We wander up and down some of the streets, checking out the campsites that range from the elaborate, like an entire structure made of PVC pipe and covered with a tarp that spans two campsites and must hold at least ten people, to the very simple, like the one that is literally just a single sleeping bag rolled out next to a Honda Civic.

Somewhere in between my thoughts and memories of Dad, last night's DMs with Jay keep creeping into my mind. If being passionate about something makes a good video, what am I passionate about? Aside from crafting, there's music and, well . . . my family, obviously. Everything I am working toward right now is about them. My dad's legacy, making my mom proud, staying close to my brother. So how I can translate any of that into a video filmed at Cabazon?

What would Dad do?

Dad would talk to people. That was his thing, and he passed that thing on to me. Dad had this great segment on his morning show called *Sam on the Streets*, because his name was Sam, and it was like a radio version of *Humans of New York* that was usually funny but sometimes poignant and moving. He'd approach people at shopping centers, the beach, wherever, and ask them truly random questions, like, "What would you do if you found a penguin in your freezer?" and somehow that would lead to the people spilling their guts to him, telling their most wonderful stories. Stories about their lives and their hopes and dreams and unbelievable things that they had been through. On his most famous segment, a woman broke into tears talking about a baby she gave up for adoption twenty years before, and the baby, who was now grown up, obviously, ended up recognizing the story when she heard it on the radio, and she called in, and they were reunited. Everyone loved *Sam on the Streets*, especially me and Jordan. So here I am racking my brain for engaging entertainment content when I really need to look no farther than my dad, especially on this day when I'm doing nothing but thinking about him. This is my moment to channel him, be Andi on the Avenue or something, and try out his interviews.

So, vlog camera out and rolling, I stop every now and then to talk to different campers myself. Jordan films while I ask some of the exact random questions Dad loved—"What is your opinion on garden gnomes?" and "What's the first thing that comes to your mind when you hear the word *fidget*?" and "When is the last time you vomited and why?" But instead of the interesting, amusing, surprising answers my dad was able to draw out of people, I'm met with nothing but strained, stilted replies. The whole experience is uncomfortable, awkward, and downright boring for everyone involved.

And I'm not just disappointed, I'm angry. I'm good at talking to people. Jordan gets so annoyed with me because I'll chat up everyone I meet—the guy waiting next to us at Starbucks, the family at the crosswalk. I even stay after class to talk more to my teachers. This whole interview thing should come easy. It's in my blood.

"This is a complete failure," I say after we talk to a lanky white guy who doesn't even know what the word *fidget* means, and we decide it's time to go into the festival grounds. "I suck at this. I might as well put some white noise in the background of this video and promote it as a sleep aid."

"Stop interviewing boring people, then." Jordan shrugs out this suggestion as if all of this is just that easy. Interviewing people. Filming some kind of video that is completely out of my comfort zone. Coming up with all this money to pay for college. *It's easy, Andi. Why haven't you just done the easy thing yet?*

I let out a long sigh. "It's not their fault; it's me. I guess I'm not Dad. I can't pull off these interviews." Maybe it *is* easy and, and I can't even handle this simple thing.

"We'll try again later," Jordan says, like that, too, will be easy. "I think you just need some sustenance first." He grabs me by the elbow and, of course, drags me to the nearest Spice Pie stand.

Happy for something else to focus my attention on for the time being, I shake off my self-doubt and grin up at my brother. "Do you realize that, aside from breakfast burritos and random treats, Spice Pie is officially the only thing we've eaten since we've been here?"

"Fine by me," Jordan says as he shoves a slice into his mouth.

Finally we get a text from Hipster Matthew and head back to the meeting spot. Today he has traded in his Crocs for a fedora.

"You could interview this guy about his fashion choices," Jordan says quietly.

"Hey, now." I elbow him. "Don't speak ill of Hipster Matthew. He charges our phones, and he gives us free things, and he will hopefully provide us with an exclusive interview with the Known that will go viral and launch my channel to internet notoriety and provide a steady income stream so I can go to college with you. Hipster Matthew is our friend. Our ridiculous, slightly awkward friend. Could he use a makeover? Yes. Do we love him anyway? Also yes."

We walk up to him and his fedora, and he gives us a fist pound in greeting, chatting with us for a bit about what we've been up to at the festival while we wait for everyone to show up.

"I think the best band I saw yesterday was the Gold Parade," he says. Suddenly Hipster Matthew gets a tiny bit cooler.

"Andi loves them," Jordan says.

"They're local to us," I tell him. "Pasadena band. They played in the parking lot of our mall once."

Hipster Matthew is impressed.

Quan shows up sans Dan again (he's checking out Blood Red Riot at the Main Stage), wearing another

T-shirt with a video game joke I don't get and a hat pulled down low over his head. He fills me in on all the amenities provided by his hotel until the Cs, who are genuinely the nicest people I've ever met, join in the conversation, then Sadie, who is wearing the tiniest sundress and the hugest hat ever, and finally Jay and Dev.

Jay smiles at me as soon as he walks up. It's not the big smile he gives to everyone, it's a smile with a secret. A smile that's a reminder of how we left things between the two of us last night, and a reminder that we're going to meet up later. It's a smile that cuts right through me in an unexpected way.

I smile back, trying to return the same sort of vibe. But my smile is dead upon arrival when it's met with Dev's glare. I wonder if Dev told his brother about our encounter this morning. Given Jay's smile, and the way he's looking at me right now, he either didn't hear about it or he simply doesn't care.

"Okay, people," Hipster Matthew says, clapping once to get our attention. I break eye contact with Jay and turn back to the fedora. "Today's scavenger hunt task is a little bit different. There are two parts. Part one, you have a riddle to solve. Once you figure it out, part two, you need to spell out the answer to the riddle by taking pictures of letters around the festival. No two letters can be from the same place, and only one letter can be from a sign on a food stand. Once you have all the letters, use the photo collage app on your loaner phone to arrange them so they spell out the answer. Then upload, hashtag, and come back to check in. First person with the riddle answered and photographed, then the answer spelled out in letters, collaged, uploaded, and then checked in is the winner. Got it?"

"Got it," says Sadie. She exudes confidence, while I'm wondering how difficult this riddle is going to be. If it has to do with bands playing at the festival, Jay and I seem to have an advantage over the rest, although Quan definitely knows a lot of the DJs and electronic acts over on the Palm Tree Stage that I've never heard of, and he could probably shoot a quick text to Dan, who seems to be a superfan of every band on the lineup, for anything else. If it's a random question, though, I might get a little stuck. I've never been great at riddles, and Jordan is more of a math-minded person, so word stuff isn't really his bag.

"Okay, here are the phones. I'll give you all the same ones you had yesterday." He passes out our loaner phones. I open all my apps and see that I'm still signed in to everything, so I find the photo collage app to make sure it's easy to use.

"Anyone want me to charge for you while you're out?" We all hand over our phones and backup battery packs, and Matthew heads off to Mobilocity's magic charging land, leaving us alone again.

Jordan leans into my ear. "Don't freak about this riddle. I doubt it's going to be too complex. They don't want to waste all of our time at the festival on some unsolvable puzzle. They want us hashtagging as much as possible, not pissed because we can't figure it out."

"You're right," I say, taking a deep breath. "We got this."

I'm itching to go talk to Jay and see if we can pick up today where we left off last night, or if what his brother said to me is going to make things weird between us now. Aside from the fact that his brother is even more of a d-bag than anyone should be allowed to be, I didn't make any startling discoveries about Jay this morning, so that's a good sign. But I see him playing with his loaner phone and something in me, some gut instinct, tells me to hold off until after today's scavenger hunt.

So instead of walking over to Jay, I grab Jordan and drag him over to talk to Sadie. We ask her what bands she saw yesterday and how she liked them. When she mentions that she saw the Gold Parade at my recommendation, I don't bring up Jay and she doesn't mention him.

"So, did they turn you into a music fan?" I ask. "I'll be personally offended if they didn't."

"I actually liked them more than anything else I saw." Sadie twirls the lighter ends of her long hair around her finger. "I just tagged along here with my neighbor and her friends, and they're more into the DJs and stuff. I spent most of the night at that Palm Tree Stage, and, not gonna lie, I'm dreading going back there. The *unce-unce-unce* music really isn't my scene."

Jordan doesn't hesitate. "You can hang out with us when you get over them. Let me give you my number."

Hipster Matthew has her real phone, so Jordan actually writes his number on her arm with a pen from her bag. As he does it, I smile over at Jay as if to say, *My brother is shooting his shot.*

He smiles back and shakes his head. And his smile seems to say, *I'm not here for her, anyway.*

Finally, Hipster Matthew comes back with the day's challenge. "Remember, everyone," he says, adjusting his fedora, "the goal for today is to explore the festival and have fun. The directions are on the cards, along with reminders about the rules. First one back here with everything complete wins five points as well as today's prize—a portable Mobilocity charger and a one-hundred-dollar Visa gift card to use on anything you want. Okay, everybody ready?"

We all nod, and I grab Jordan's arm and squeeze.

"All righty." Hipster Matthew passes out the cards facedown, then turns on his camera, ready to get us in action. "And . . . go!"

I flip over our card, and Jordan and I bring our heads together over it.

What falls but doesn't break &
what breaks but doesn't fall—
here at the festival?

Jordan and I look at each other. "I have no idea what this means," I say, and he shrugs.

A quick glance at the other teams shows Cody and Corey still studying their card, Quan already gone, Sadie poking at her loaner phone, and Jay and his brother arguing over something. Of course.

"Let's get out of sight," I whisper to Jordan. "We'll put some distance between us and everyone else and figure it out without everyone watching."

He nods, and we walk as quickly as we can over to the next art installation, a huge computer screen with changing pictures from festivalgoers who used the official Cabazon hashtag. We duck behind it and start talking out the riddle.

"Okay, first of all, is this one thing or two things we're looking for?" I ask.

Jordan points at the card. "It's weird they used that *and* sign . . . What's that called again?"

"Ampersand. Yeah, I wonder if it means something that they used that instead of spelling out the word *and*."

"Look it up!"

"Isn't that cheating?" I want to win, but not like that.

"He didn't say not to. And who's going to know? Here, give me the phone."

Jordan quickly types the riddle into the search bar. "There's only an answer to the first part. What falls and doesn't break, and what breaks and doesn't fall, the answer is night and day. Oh, I get it. Nightfall. Daybreak."

I lean over his shoulder to see the phone screen. "This doesn't use the ampersand, though. And what does the whole thing mean? Night and day at the festival? I don't get it."

"Do we spell out night and day and hope for the best?"

"Wait! The festival app. Pull it up. Search through all the bands. There! Stop!" Sure enough, one of the first bands to play on the Cactus Stage today is called Nightz & Dayz.

"Boom! Let's do this!"

We run off through the festival taking photos of the letters that spell out the band's name. We pay tribute to our favorite food by using our one food stand letter on the *i* from the Spice Pie sign. We gather a *D* from an LA Dodgers T-shirt, an *N* from a pair of New Balances we spot on a dude lounging in the grass. A *y* from Hipster Matthew's own Mobilocity booth. We're almost done, with only *g*, *h*, and an ampersand to go, when I spot Jay and Dev on the other side of a crowd of people on the lawn in front of the Outdoor Stage.

"I want to go see what they're doing."

"Andi, don't worry about them. We're almost done. Let's just finish."

"It will only take a second."

Attempting my best stealth maneuvers, I creep up behind the crowd of drunk twentysomething guys who are having some sort of dance party. They're moving around too much for me to stay completely hidden, and they're being way too loud and obnoxious for me to really hear what Jay and Dev are saying, but I'm able to see pretty quickly that Dev has a GoPro out and he's filming Jay.

The difference in Jay when he's on camera is obvious. His posture, the expression on his face, the way he carries his entire body. It was one thing watching it on the video earlier, but seeing it in person is eerie. It's like his body has been taken over by an alien.

A tug on my tank top sends me pitching backward, losing my balance and falling on my butt in the grass. "Stop staring," Jordan says. "Get up and let's finish so we can win this thing."

"I wasn't staring, I was—"

"You were staring. Quit lying to yourself."

"I just wanted to know why they were taking a break and filming when there is a contest to be won. I was trying to gather some intel."

"What's more important? Intel or the Known interview?"

I turn to Jay and Dev again, but they're gone. There's no sign of them. It's almost like they were never there.

"Look, I know you're in love with him—"

"Gross! No, I'm not!"

"But we have to win this! Let's go!"

Jordan and I gather our last letters. We prompt two of the drunk guys to make an *h* with their hands, find a *G* on a sticker on a girl's Hydro Flask, and realize way too late that Jordan's had an ampersand on the back of his tank top this whole time.

We collage all the photos, upload and hashtag, then run back toward our meeting spot. But as soon as it's in sight, we see Jay and Dev already there, chatting with Hipster Matthew and looking smug. Well, Dev is looking smug, anyway.

"Shit," Jordan says.

"You're second place today, team," Hipster Matthew says as we approach. "Let me see how you did."

I hand over our phone, but it doesn't matter. We didn't win. And Jay and Dev beat us. It's a double blow.

"Sucks to suck," Dev says under his breath as Hipster Matthew checks our collage.

Jay gives his brother a small shove in the side. "God, shut up, Dev."

"Just out of curiosity," Jordan asks Hipster Matthew, "about how much time did they beat us by?"

"Oh, less than a minute. They got here right before you folks did. That was a close one."

Less than a minute. Less than the time it took for me to stop and watch Jay film for his video. If I hadn't done that, if I had listened to my brother and kept my focus on the task at hand, we would have won for sure.

God, why can't I get this guy out of my head?

CHAPTER 8

>>> • <<<

"HOW ARE YOU DOING OVER HERE?"

I'm sitting on the grass toward the back of the Outdoor Stage, half listening to Future|Future, a female hip-hop duo, and trying to decompress from this nightmare day, but now Jay stands next to me, blocking the sun with his shadow.

I give him a half-hearted smile. "Eh."

"Do you mind if I join you? I'm feeling a little 'eh' myself."

I shrug and pat the grass next to me. Jay lowers himself, crossing his legs.

"Where's your brother?" he asks.

I nod to the left, where Jordan sits with Sadie, deep in conversation about something or other; it's like they don't even realize Future|Future is onstage fifty yards in front of them.

"Where's yours?"

"Who cares." He rolls his eyes. "I'm sorry about earlier."

I give him another half smile. "Thanks for the apology," I say. "But there's no need. You guys won fair and square. Nothing to be sorry for."

"I know." He lets out a long sigh. "I'm sorry about Dev, like, in general, though. I've been wanting to talk to you about him, but I haven't really had a chance."

"What is there to say?" I reach in front of my legs and start picking blades of grass and shredding them.

"That my brother has always been a jerk. That's just how he is. To everyone. It's not only to you. It's to me and to literally everyone we meet. Always."

"Aw, and I thought I was special."

He laughs. "But this is what I wanted to tell you yesterday. My brother, he writes all my videos. The person I am on those videos, I'm reading a script that he writes. What you see on the screen is his personality, not mine."

This is certainly in line with what I've learned about both Jay and Dev over the course of the weekend so far, and what I've seen when Jay is on camera. But, still. "Why? I don't get it."

He nods toward Future|Future on the stage. "Do you like them?"

"They're okay. I like their song that's on the radio right now, but I don't know too much about their other stuff."

"Want to go for a walk?"

"Why not?"

Jay hops up, then reaches out his hand to help me

up. I consider taking it, but instead I push myself off the grass and brush off the back of my shorts. "Let me tell my brother where I'm going."

Jordan looks up as I approach and shoots me a back-off-I'm-busy look, which I immediately dismiss with a head shake.

"I'm going for a walk with Jay. Text me if you need anything or go anywhere."

"Okay, I will. Be back for Tarot Card."

"I will. And I know you won't text me." I kick him lightly on his leg. "But I need to say it anyway."

"I'll make sure he does," Sadie says, smiling up at me. Then she turns to my brother, her eyes narrowed, and shoves him playfully on the shoulder. "Why wouldn't you let your sister know where you are? That's rude."

"Thanks for looking out, Sadie. See you later."

Jay and I wander off into the festival, not really sure where we're going. I'm aware of the space between us—a polite distance, but close enough that you can tell we're together. Well, not *together* together, but with each other. Close enough that he could reach out and grab my hand. Close enough that he might accidentally brush against my bare leg.

Not that I want him to do those things or anything. Nope.

"My brother never had a lot of friends growing up," Jay says finally, as we walk through a gazebo set up in the middle of the lawn, black flowers covering the top and dripping down the sides. "I don't know if he just didn't know how to do the friend thing or if he never met the right people or what, but he was always a little bit of a loner. I used to think he wanted to be alone and he liked it that way, but I've realized more and more that it wasn't really a choice."

I nod. Already I have a lot to say in response. *I can see why* or *this is no excuse to be such a jerk* or some other little quip. But I decide to just keep my smart-ass comments to myself for the time being and let Jay tell his story.

"Dude! Jay Bankar!"

So much for Jay telling his story. We both turn around and see two white guys I can only describe as dudebros trotting up to meet us.

"I told you it was him," the taller one with the sideways Pabst Blue Ribbon hat says, reaching out to slap hands with Jay in that overcomplicated guy way. "Big fans of your channel, man."

Of course they are.

The shorter one with the low V-neck T-shirt repeats the hand-slapping ritual. "How's your grandma doing, dude? She even speak to you anymore?"

Jay slips his fake face on like a Halloween mask. "Ah, Grandma's cool. She knows how it is." He laughs in this douchey way, and I must have an aneurysm because I completely black out while they take a selfie together, then chuckle and hand slap and make grunting noises or whatever.

Finally the guys leave, but not before the shorter one turns around and shouts, "I sure hope I don't see this chick in your next video! Har har har!" Yes, he literally says *har har har*, and then he has the audacity to wink at me.

It's possible I may hate Jay's fans more than his actual channel.

"Sorry," he says, aggressively avoiding eye contact.

"What—and I cannot stress this enough—the hell was that?"

"Just some fans," he mumbles to the ground. The more he tries to pretend this repulsive fan encounter never happened, obviously, the more I'm going to give him shit about it.

"So, you want to go hang out with those really awesome guys? They seem so fun. Want me to call them back over here?" I wave at the retreating forms of the dudebros and yell out, "Hey! Guys!"

"Oh my God, Andi, no!" He lunges for my arm, yanking it down. The contact, his hand on my skin, even for this quick moment, burns in the best way. He pulls away as quickly as he grabbed me, and I miss the feeling of his hand on me immediately. I don't want him to know how much I liked it, so I do my best to keep the playful mocking going, even though I'm a little bit distracted.

"Oh, so you're too good for your fans, then?" I play-fully elbow him in the side so I can get another touch in.

He mockingly rolls his eyes at me. "Don't say it like that. I took a picture with them, didn't I? It's just that, well, I hope it's pretty obvious that I wouldn't actu-ally be friends with those guys. Now, Dev, on the other hand . . ."

"Well, it looks like I could have taken a picture of you for the scavenger hunt yesterday, Mr. Celebrity."

"It's not like that." His fingers repeatedly curl in and flex out as we continue our walk. "And you're not going to be in my next video. I promise."

"You wouldn't want me to steal the show, huh?"

That gets a laugh out of him. "Now, what were we talking about?"

"Your brother's villain origin story."

"Oh, yeah. So, he started hanging out online a lot, and he found these message boards where he finally made friends. My parents were actually excited. My mom has monthly happy hours with the women on her parenting message board. And my dad is the moderator on some Lord of the Rings chat. They both love that shit, so they were really happy that Dev finally found 'a community of like-minded people.'" He makes air quotes with his fingers. "Those were their exact words.

"The thing is, though, these like-minded people are not nice." We hop out of the way of a string of girls holding hands, the girl in the front leading the rest of them toward their next stage or back to their camp or somewhere else fun as they all sing the Known's latest hit. "This message board is a big collection of assholes being assholes to one another and other people. And the longer my brother was on there, the more he changed from being this quiet guy who kept to himself into the lovely specimen you see before you today.

"Anyway, he's a smart guy, and through his online group, he recognized a niche for this type of humor, so he had me film some videos with his jokes and ideas."

"Why didn't he just do it himself? I mean, that seems like a pretty big thing for you to do for him."

"Honestly? Dev tried at first, but he's just terrible on camera. He had me try it out, since I was just sitting around the house, bored, and I didn't think anyone would see them, so I didn't see any harm in it. It turns out I'm way better at the whole on-screen thing. And those first few videos got a great response, so we filmed more. We eventually had a good schedule going and grew a little following, and it was all pretty fun. The focus of the videos back then was more innocent. Just observations about human nature from Dev's opinion. I'd film it and talk about it all like it was mine." He laughs. "This was last year. I was a junior. The only places I was going were baseball practice and the gelato place down the street. There was no way I was having that many opinions about anything but how much homework my math teacher was giving."

Ah, baseball. That explains the arms.

"Ooh, what's this?" Jay stops in front a canopied area filled with tables and people. A wooden sign popping out of the ground reads CAMP CABAZON, with an arrow pointing to a table manned by a tall Asian girl in a neon pink bikini and Uggs. "Is this an arts and crafts tent?"

I break into a jumpy clap—an automatic response when presented with the possibility of getting my art on. "Crafts!" I'm so excited to check out the tent that I impulsively grab Jay's arm and pull him to the info table. I realize too late what I've done, and I drop his arm as quickly as I grabbed it, but the damage has been done. More touching. God, what's wrong with me?

"I'm sorry," I say to Jay. "Can we check it out while we talk? I didn't know this was here."

"Anything to see you get this excited." His voice has a hint of playfulness to it, but he doesn't sound sarcastic. It's like he really is happy to see me get excited about something, which makes my skin break out in tingles. Before I have a chance to dwell on the tingle outbreak, we're interrupted by Bikini-and-Ugg Girl.

"Welcome to Camp Cabazon," she says, smiling at us. "I'm Mimi. Are you ready to get crafty?"

I rub my hands together. "I'm always ready, Mimi." It's no secret that my happy place is alone in my room scouring Pinterest for a craft project while my music is blasting. And the truth is, the end product doesn't even matter all that much, which is why I have videos on my channel about everything from bullet journaling to embroidery. What gets me going is the act of creation. And even producing the videos is an act of creation that I love. There's something so satisfying about taking hours of messy footage and turning it into this slick finished product that tells a story. But I get that same satisfaction from almost anything I make. So, I don't even know what kind of crafts lie beyond this threshold, but I legit don't even care.

"Feel free to explore the camp tent." Mimi waves her arm out to the collection of small tables behind her. "Some of the crafts are free, and some, like the ceramics painting table and the basket weaving, have a small fee. The camp counselor at each table will give you all the details."

My impulse is to hug Mimi, but I rein it in and smile and wave instead, then I assume Jay follows me as I bounce into the tent to see what options are available.

"Look! Crochet! And coloring books." My head is on a swivel, turning every which way like an owl's, taking in all the tables and their wooden signs explaining what crafty treasure awaits at each one. "Oh, there's the ceramics painting. That looks super fun, but I don't want to pay for anything."

Jay catches up to me and shakes his head, letting out a small laugh. "Man, you're so excited about this."

I stop and turn to face him, my hands on my hips. "Are you laughing at me?"

"Absolutely not. Your enthusiasm is contagious, actually."

"Good. Because I have no time for people who laugh at me."

We walk through the tent, scoping out the various arts and crafts options, but before I can really get a good look around, we're spotted.

"Andi! Jay!"

Panic shoots through me instantly. Is this another one of Jay's gross fans who also happens to watch my channel, too? Sure, Jay is growing on me, and even giving me a few tingly feelings, but that doesn't mean I'm emotionally prepared for a picture of us together showing up on someone's story. My eyes shoot around the tent, but there's nowhere to hide unless I literally duck under one of the tables on my hands and knees like it's an earthquake drill at school.

But the panic rushes out of me just as quickly when I see it's Cody and Corey, wearing their matching shirts and casually decoupaging small cardboard boxes. Obviously Jay and I don't have fans in common. My small group of crafty viewers have much better taste than that.

"Hey, you two!" I stand next to the pair as Jay turns the

chair next to them backward and sits down. "Whatcha making?"

Cody holds up her box and cocks her head as she examines it. "Jewelry boxes? I think? I had a grand vision, but it's losing something in the execution."

"What are you two up to?" Corey asks as he cuts a headline out of an old *Rolling Stone* to add to his box. "Joining forces to dominate the scavenger hunt and split the prizes?"

"That would actually be a good idea." I nudge Jay's shoulder with my elbow. "What do you think? Sneak attack tomorrow?"

Jay lets out a sharp humorless laugh. "Oh, my brother would love that."

I sit down at one of the empty chairs and begin absently flipping through an old issue of *Teen Vogue* on the table. "Are you recording an episode of your podcast this weekend?"

"Nah," Corey says as he sorts through his cutouts. "We're just here to have fun."

"We thought about it, but we're all about books, so we couldn't really think of anything to relate to." Cody smiles at me, as if she can see into my brain and understands the turmoil I'm having about my own channel. Is she psychic? "We brought a few books with us to take some pictures for our feed, but besides that, it's just not 'our brand.'" She says those last two words in the most perfect Matthew voice, and I can't help but laugh.

"Are you doing something?" she asks me.

I chew on my bottom lip as I try to decide how much I want to reveal to her and, by extension, to Jay, who is standing right behind me. "Kinda. I don't know. I'm thinking about . . . expanding my reach somehow."

Jay's surprise is palpable. "Like moving away from crafting? Why? You haven't stopped smiling since we found this crafting tent."

But I'm saved from explaining myself by Cody, who says, "I've actually watched some of your videos before, Andi."

"You have?"

"I followed your crochet tutorial to make a blanket for my grandma for her birthday. She totally loved it." She pulls out her phone, finds the pictures of the blanket, made with a rich turquoise yarn, which turned out really beautiful, and she shows them to me, full of pride. Her smile as she swipes through the pictures warms me up from the inside, sending bursts of joy all through my body.

Wow. I have a fan, too. I mean, I knew that people liked my tutorials. Unlike most of the rest of YouTube, my comments are almost always positive and thankful, peppered with the occasional spam comment about making $10K per month by working from home. But if you compare that with the comments on, well, almost any other video, it's a breath of fresh air. So I knew I was creating something that was useful, something that was helping people on some level.

But there's something so fulfilling about someone who looks you in the eye and tells you that they appreciate what you put out there. That what you do matters.

"What about you, Jay?" Corey says, snapping me out of my thoughts. "Are you making a video this weekend?"

Jay leans over, resting his hands on the back of the chair I'm sitting in. "We filmed something on the drive down here. I told Dev that was all we were doing unless we win the interview with the Known."

Corey's mouth flattens into a straight line. "Your brother is, uh . . ."

"I know. He's a dick. Sorry about that. I feel like I should be wearing a T-shirt this weekend that says SORRY ABOUT MY BROTHER." He laughs, but it's one of those laughs you force out when you're aware that what you're saying is only funny because it's absolutely true.

"Well, we're going to go," I say. "I need to explore this tent and find something to craft."

"You should do a video in here," Cody says, laughing and holding up her box. "I could use your help with this situation, honestly."

We say goodbye and make our way from table to table, checking out the offerings. But I don't get far before my eyes land on something that, damn, must be some kind of sign.

"Dude! Friendship bracelets!" I tug on the side of Jay's tank top. "Are you down?" How is it that the exact craft I was working on at home is waiting for me here as I try to determine my next step?

"I'm so down," Jay says, and we make our way to the table. There's a Black guy sitting there, arms covered in colorful bracelets, playing with his phone, and he pulls out one of his AirPods when we approach and introduces himself as Patrick, a Camp Cabazon counselor.

"All the colors of embroidery floss are in the bins in front of you. Here's a paper with directions on making different patterns, and you can use those binder clips stuck to the table to clamp your bracelet down."

Jay takes two directions papers from Patrick and hands me one, but I hand it right back. "I won't be needing this, Patrick. You can save it for someone else."

Patrick laughs, and Jay snorts in approval. "Expert level. I love it." Patrick pushes a stack of small bins toward us. "Let me know if you have any questions. But it sounds like you have it handled." Then he winks at me and puts his AirPod back in, turning his attention back to his phone.

"Okay, I'm going to teach you how to do this," I say to Jay.

"Just like one of your videos?"

"Yup. In fact, I was actually in the middle of filming a friendship bracelet video right when we got these tickets. We got sidetracked by packing, and I never finished it."

"Well," he says, "let's finish it now. Teach me your crafty ways, wise one."

My cheeks flush with heat. "You want me to film myself teaching you to make a friendship bracelet?" I know I put my videos on the internet for anyone to see, but there's something so personal about giving Jay a one-on-one tutorial, showing him that unedited side of myself.

"Sure. And so does Cody. You heard her, right? Do you have your camera?" He smiles as he pokes my BeDazzled belt bag, where my vlog camera and clip-on ring light are tucked away. "Did you make this? I like it."

"Of course I did. I can make you one if you want. I can put a sparkly poop emoji right here, just for you."

"Hmm. I don't know if it's my style. Friendship bracelets are much more my jam."

I pull out my camera and turn it over in my hands as I consider Jay's idea. "Well, I can't use this for my channel, but what the hell. Let's do it."

"Why can't you use it?" Jay seems genuinely baffled, and I can't help but laugh.

"Just because you have a ton of subscribers, that doesn't mean you're a draw, buddy. I'm trying to beef up my viewership here, not drive everyone away."

"Um, have you seen my face?" He cups his hands around his chin and blinks innocently at me.

"Um, have you seen your fans?"

"Fine. Whatever. I don't even care if you use it. I just want to see you in action."

I know my cheeks are flushed again, because he keeps saying these things that hit me in just the right spot inside, so I turn my focus to my camera to keep Jay from seeing how affected I am by his attention. I test a few angles, looking for some good light, and I finally prop the camera on top of a few embroidery floss boxes and balance it against the wooden table sign.

"Hi, everyone," I say, waving into the lens. "Today I'm here at the Cabazon Valley Music and Arts Festival with YouTube's bad boy Jay Bankar, and I'm going to teach this monster how to make a friendship bracelet. Who knows, maybe he can use it to make an actual friend and stop being such a pile of garbage on the internet."

"Ouch," Jay says, smiling. He looks into the camera and shakes his head. "Hi, everyone. I wonder if it's too late to get out of this. Send help?" It's a relief to see that he doesn't slip into his fake face when my camera is pointed at him. He's relaxed and comfortable, and looks like himself. Like the guy I've gotten to know over the past few days. Like the guy I am actually enjoying being with.

"Nope. It was your idea, but this is my video, so we

do this my way. Okay, the first thing we need to do for friendship bracelets is get some embroidery floss from a craft store like Michaels and pick out a color palette." I rummage through the provided stash in the box I don't have my camera sitting on top of and eventually decide on light and dark shades of pink and purple. "Your friendship bracelets don't need to match your outfits. Think about colors that make you happy or that symbolize important things in your life—school colors or sports teams, for example. Today I'm doing pink and purple because they match the Cabazon logo." As Jay digs through the bin, I grab scissors from the table, measure out my embroidery floss, tie it off, and clamp it on to the table, explaining the steps to the camera as I go along. Jay finally decides on black, white, and gray, "To match my dark soul," he says, and I help him get his bracelet started.

"You clearly never went to summer camp," I say, trying to untangle his mess. "You want your knots to be nice and tight. Like your abs."

"You've been checking out my abs, eh?"

I wink at him. "See how a series of nice tight knots starts to form a cool pattern?" I angle my bracelet up toward my camera.

Jay angles his bracelet up to the camera, too. "I need some practice," he says. "Good thing I ran into you here, Andi. My friendship bracelet game is weak."

We're at the part of bracelet making where we just keep doing it for a while, and most of this will get cut or sped up, so I don't have anything to say to the camera— I'll just overdub this with my quick instructions during editing. And I'm not going to actually use any of this on my channel anyway, so after a small stretch of silence, it feels like a good time to ease back into the conversation we were having before we stumbled upon the Camp Cabazon tent.

"So, do you want to finish this Dev story?" I peek over to his friendship bracelet and see that his knots are loose and crooked, but he doesn't seem to care. He keeps going with confident enthusiasm, like he's some kind of human golden retriever.

"Oh, yes," he says. "Back to Dev. I was talking about how the videos started getting popular. Then he kept trying to be edgier, so he added more of his humor. His humor, of course, had evolved into being as much of an asshole as possible at all times."

"Yeah, it's really bad. I mean, really bad."

"I know," he says, letting out a resigned sigh. "It wasn't this bad at first, but he kept going for it to draw a reaction out of people, and it got worse and worse. We did one prank video, and it went viral. The rest is history."

"So why did you go along with it?"

He stops his knotting and looks away, then back at me. Something dark crosses his face, as if whatever is coming up is painful for him. "Money."

Oof. That word lands right in my gut. "What do you mean?"

"My brother and I need the money. Well, I do. I did something pretty dumb. I met these guys at VidCon last year, and they convinced me to invest in their production company. I was young and stupid, and they totally sold me. I had Dev withdraw almost all the money my parents put aside for me for college from this joint account that Dev has had access to since he turned eighteen. Of course, the guys were total scam artists, and I lost all the money. My parents found out, obviously, and they were furious, so I had to find some way to pay them back. This was right around the time our first prank video went viral, and we realized we could make real money. With every stupid prank, we got more views and more ad revenue. Every hate-watch by you and everyone else puts money back in that account and makes me a little less of a disappointment to my parents. Every time someone shares a video and says, 'Can you believe how awful this guy is?' is another semester of a college education I'll be able to pay for again. And I know you think Dev is the worst, and he is, kinda. But he's also doing all of this just to help me. He keeps a little bit of the money for himself, but it's mostly just for me. He writes and films and produces, and all I have to do is be awful on camera. And the more awful I am, the closer I get to paying off this dumb mistake."

My mouth hangs open slightly at his story, and how similar it is to my own. Here I was worried about making a video about fashion and feeling like a sellout, and this guy is being a total dumpster fire with no qualms and raking in the cash. I'm going to need a minute to process all of this.

"But aren't you—" I grapple for the right words. *Aren't you embarrassed? Aren't you disappointed in yourself? Doesn't it make you feel dirty?* But I don't even need to finish, because he seems to get what I'm after and answers immediately.

"Oh, yeah. I was never proud of myself, and I was pretty pissed we had started doing it with my real name. Suddenly everyone at my school knew about the videos, and even though people loved them, they all thought that was the real me. Even friends I'd had forever who knew it was all a script. Perception is reality, right?" He rolls the embroidery floss that hangs loose at the end of his bracelet between his fingers. "My girlfriend even broke up with me."

"Why don't you stop?"

"I can't." He looks up from his bracelet, and he scoots his chair closer to me. He lowers his voice and leans in, like he's sharing a secret. "I'm so close to making it all back. Dev thinks this interview with the Known could get us there. And it's easy money, really. We make a video a week, which we film all day on Saturday and he edits all day on Sunday. I make more money than anyone else I know. Once the college money is all in my account, I'm going to start saving for a new car." He leans back in the chair again, tilting his head to the sky. "You probably don't understand this, but I *need* the money. For college. For my parents."

His words suck all the air out of the tent, and I have to scoot away just a bit to give myself space from this reality. Don't understand it? I'm living it.

I pull in a long breath and let out my question, quiet and slow. A question that might sound judgy, but is just as judgy toward me as it is toward him. "And the money makes doing awful things worth it?" I was never considering throwing all my morals out the door for ad revenue, but there is a reason that none of my video ideas this weekend have worked for me. They're not *me*. I need to know how much that matters.

"I know it sounds terrible, but . . ."

Turning my focus down to my bracelet, I stare at the colorful thread knotted in a complicated diamond pattern instead of Jay's too-hot face, which has tightened with the weight of everything he's admitting to me. "I know money can justify a lot of things. I actually understand that more than you realize." I mean, that's exactly why I'm here, but I'm not ready to share that with him just yet. "But you're putting some real trash out into the world. Making money off making fun of people? It's just so . . . gross. I started watching your most recent video, the one where you call some girl that you hit on in the first place a dumb bitch, and—"

"Hold on," he says. "Okay, let's talk about this. First of all, I don't love that particular video, but it was sponsored."

"What do you mean?"

"The Coffee Coffin paid me money to say their name on camera a certain number of times, go into their store, order a drink, and talk about how good it was. It was basically a commercial for them. I acted like a dick to their employee, who was nothing but professional the entire time. And I sure did love that delicious Coffee Coffin latte, which is all that really matters, I guess."

"But that girl—"

"Andrea is my neighbor. She's been begging me to be in one my videos for the past four months. She thought it was hilarious. You know that video with my grandma? It was *her* idea. She sent it to all her friends back in India; they all think she's famous now. So, like, it's all trash. I get it. But it's not all *my* trash." His voice is pleading, like he's trying to convince me. Or himself.

"Of course it is. It has your name and your face on it," I say. "That makes it yours."

"Ugh," he says, dropping the friendship bracelet

to rub his hands over his face. "This probably sounds dumb, but I tell myself it's like being an actor. It's just a part. Someone has to play the villain, right?"

I shake my head. "Whatever helps you sleep at night, my dude."

"What do you mean?"

"Come on. You know you're not playing this like the villain at all. You play Jay Bankar like some kind of d-bag dudebro hero. And people look to you as a hero. Fake or not, your viewers take what you say as if it's good and right. You read your comments. You saw those guys earlier. You know that's true." I bump him lightly on his shoulder for emphasis, and he looks directly in my eyes when I do it.

The eye contact sends a jolt all through me. Electricity down to my toes.

Does he feel that, too?

If he does, his face doesn't give it away. The tightness from earlier is gone now, leaving him looking sad and exhausted. Worn out. "I don't want to be this person, Andi," he says finally, his shoulders slumping slightly.

But I still feel that crackle of electricity between us.

"Can I tell you something?" he asks, picking up his bracelet again.

"Um. Sure."

"That look on your face yesterday morning after you

realized who I was? I hated it. It made me sick to see you look at me that way."

I want to ask him why. I want so badly to hear him tell me why, but I can't bring the word out of my mouth. It's just one little word, but my insides twist up at the thought of actually asking him, and then of hearing his answer. So instead I say, "But you loved the way those fans of yours earlier looked at you, right?"

He laughs, and it's like I dumped a bucket of water on the crackling flame of tension between us.

"You're lucky you don't have to worry about money," he says, relaxing back into the chair.

"Why do you keep saying that? You don't know that."

"But you do this for fun." He waves his hand around the tent at all the craft tables. "You love crafts, and you get to make videos geeking out about crafts, and it's all so wholesome."

I snort. "Wholesome doesn't pay the bills. When is the last time you saw a video about embroidery go viral?"

"But who cares about going viral?

"Um, you do?" I laugh, and it makes him smile. God, that smile could knock me right out of this chair if I let it. *Focus, Andi.* "Look, you're not the only one with money problems, okay? I'm supposed to be filming some kind of attention-grabbing video this weekend that will take my channel in a new direction and get me more subscribers so I can start making money on ad revenue, but nothing is working for me. I have a bunch of B-roll and boring, unusable interviews and nothing else."

"So that's what you were talking about earlier? What kind of new direction?" He sounds so interested that I hate to disappoint him with the truth.

"I have absolutely no idea. I thought it would just *come to me* when I got here, but it turns out that's not really a solid plan."

"Ah, so this is why you want the interview, huh?

"Yeah. But even if I get it, and it gets me views, where do I take my channel from there? Do I start doing . . . what, band interviews? I love music, but . . ." *But I'm not my dad.*

A silence falls between us after I trail off. The conversation had been so awesome, had made me feel so close to Jay and had made me really start to understand him. I felt so good about where we were going that of course thoughts of Dad had to creep back in to remind me that today is supposed to suck. That every single day without him is supposed to suck. Guilt stabs me right in the heart for going so long without thinking about him. *I didn't forget about you, Dad,* I say to him in my head as tears prick my eyes. I fight them back with a deep breath and, anxious to get things back to normal before Jay notices my weirdness, I turn my attention back to the camera and switch my video voice back on. "When your bracelet gets to your desired length, all you have to do is tie it off. You'll want to measure it first, just to make sure it's not too short." I wrap it around my wrist, then tie it. "Just one big knot with all the thread, like this. Then cut off the excess, and you have the perfect gift to give a friend."

When I turn to Jay to see if I pulled off my turn-around, he's shaking his head.

"What?"

"I forgot you were filming," he says, smiling.

"Well, I was. How is your bracelet coming along?"

He lifts it up to show the knotted, lumpy, half-finished mess to the camera, and this time I shake my head.

"It's a work in progress," he says, smiling even bigger. I try to smile back, but I can tell it's half-hearted.

He cocks his head to the side. "What's wrong?"

"Oh," I say. "Nothing. Well, it's not nothing. It's just . . . today has been a lot."

"Listen," he says, spreading his hand out on the table in front of him. "About the scavenger hunt—"

"Oh, no. Not that. I mean, it's that. And this conversation. And my brother." I jerk my head in the direction of where we came from earlier. "And your brother, and—"

"Wait. My brother? What does he have to do with anything? I mean, aside from what I just told you. And aside from him being a complete tool in general."

I tilt my head at him. "He didn't tell you? He got in my face this morning."

"What?" He doesn't even try to keep the irritation out of his voice. "When? What did he say?"

"Early this morning when I was coming back from the shower." It's been so long since our run-in that my white-hot rage has cooled to mild annoyance. I roll my eyes and fill Jay in on the encounter I had with Dev earlier.

"You do a pretty good impersonation of my brother," Jay says, sounding impressed.

"Yeah, my idiotic-douchebag voice is pretty solid."

"I can't believe he said that to you. I'm so sorry."

I shrug. "You aren't responsible for what he does."

"I know, but it sucks. I'm associated with him, you know? It's embarrassing." He follows my lead and measures his wonky friendship bracelet around his own wrist, then ties it off. "But . . ."

"What?"

"I'm glad you didn't listen to him. About leaving me alone." He smiles at me, and my insides go molten.

"I've tried to leave you alone, like, five times since I met you. You keep following me." I wish I didn't keep making a joke or changing the subject when he says something flirty or sweet, but I just can't handle it right now. This conversation, his smile, the way he looks at me like he's actually interested in these crafts. The realization that maybe he really isn't the awful person I thought he was. It's all so much to process in the moment, and I need some time to collect my thoughts. Instead of looking back at him, I dig around the bin and pull out some more embroidery thread, this time green and yellow like the stripes on his tank top. "Now I'm going to show you how to do an arrow pattern," I say to the camera as I start in on the instructions for a new bracelet.

"It's true," he says when I'm done talking through the next steps. "I'm totally stalking you. But in a friendly way, not a creeper way. At least I hope it's coming off friendly."

I take a deep breath and let it out slowly as I work on the knots on my bracelet. "Why?"

"Why am I not doing it in a creeper way? I thought the general rule was that people don't like that. I can get some tips from my brother if you want me to amp up the creep factor, though."

"No, I mean, why do you not let me leave you alone? I made it pretty clear I hated you, and I yelled at you a few times and called you some names. And refused to share my bacon."

"That bacon thing was a low blow." He clips the ends of his bracelet into an uneven line that matches the whole messy thing. "You want to know the truth?"

"Obviously. I wouldn't ask you and then want to hear a lie."

He shakes his head. "That. That right there. From the second I met you, you haven't let me get away with anything. Not a single thing. I really, really like that."

This admission of his warms me up from the inside. The fact that I'm straightforward and call it like I see it is something people seem to love or hate about me. I've lost friends over it before, but I've also made friends because of it, too. Apparently, Jay is a fan.

"Not everybody does," I say.

"Well, I do." We hold eye contact for a few seconds. His face doesn't give away what he's feeling at all, and I really hope my face doesn't give away that, while I stare at his mouth, I'm trying to keep myself from leaning over and biting it. "Can I ask you something?"

"Sure." My voice comes out breathier than I anticipated. *Jeez, Andi. Don't be so obvious.*

"Why *haven't* you listened to my brother? I mean, you made it pretty clear you hated me. Multiple times. Yet you're walking around this festival with me. Why?"

"Honestly?"

"Well, I don't want *you* to lie to *me*." He props his elbows on the table and rests his chin in his hands.

"Shut up." I elbow him in his arm, causing his own elbow to give out. "Honestly, I'm trying to figure that out myself. I try to keep hating you, and I can't seem to manage it. It's annoying as hell."

"What can I say? I'm charming?"

"Don't turn all Jay Bankar on me," I say. "I still have time to change my mind."

He gently places his hand on top of mine. "I really hope you don't," he says softly.

Don't make a joke. Don't change the subject. I don't, but I also don't know what to say or do instead, so I simply smile and hope that's enough.

"So, is that it?" Jay says, taking his hand back.

"Is what it?"

"The stuff you mentioned earlier? Is that the reason you've had that wrinkle between your eyes all day?"

I straighten up and rub on the skin between my eyes. "It's this day, actually." And here it is, the time in a conversation with someone new where I debate telling them about my dad or not. This is such a big part of who I am, especially on this day. Do I want to give that to Jay? Give him access to this part of myself? It's so personal. But, again, he gave me something personal. And he has given me no reason to not trust him. I let out a long sigh. "It's the anniversary of my dad's death."

Jay straightens up and scoots closer to me when he does it. "Oh God, Andi. I'm so sorry."

I focus intently on my bracelet knotting. "He died five years ago, and Jordan and I have a hard time with this day every year. We sort of thought getting away for the weekend might keep it from sucking so much this year, but it didn't work. Apparently suck can follow you anywhere. It's been nonstop crap since I woke up, or was woken up, actually, thanks to the dance party tent next to ours."

"Oh God. Those guys are the worst. I said I wasn't going to do a video this weekend, but I told Dev I'd be happy to prank them and not even film it." Jay laughs. "I have extra earplugs. Do you want to borrow them?"

"Oh, I have some, but I took them out last night because I was waiting for Jordan to call."

"Aaah, gotcha. So it's destined to be a bad day, huh?"

I explain how I talked to Dad this morning in an effort to turn things around. "But things always go to shit," I say. "On this day we got rear-ended while driving home from school, and once a few years ago Jordan was accused of shoplifting at Target and was detained by security for two hours before they figured out they had the wrong guy. And then today? It wasn't one big thing, even. Just everything. It's one of those things where nothing ever goes right."

Jay tilts his head, his face serious and his gaze intense. "Nothing?"

I shake my head. "There has never been a thing that happened on this day that is any good. Ever."

He leans closer, bringing his hand up to my face. His fingers slowly move my hair off my cheek, which he grazes lightly with his thumb. "Andi," he says, lowering his voice, "I really want to ask you something right now."

My cheek is on fire from his touch, and while he was talking, I shifted myself toward him and scooted my chair closer.

"I want you to have my friendship bracelet. Will you wear it?" He lifts his wonky, crooked bracelet from the table and presents it to me, hope in his eyes.

A loud laugh escapes my mouth. "I'd be honored." I hold my arm out to him so he can tie the bracelet on my wrist.

He smiles as he works the threads into a knot, somehow managing the task without coming into contact with my skin at all, and when he's done, he directs that smile right at me. "Does this mean we're friends now?"

"No," I say, and his face falls slightly. I tie off and cut the green and yellow bracelet I've been working on, the one that matches his shirt, and I dangle it in front of his face. "We aren't friends until you wear mine, too."

"Well, give it to me, then," he says, grabbing at the dangling bracelet. I try to tie it around his wrist, but since I measured it on my own small arm, it's way too short to fit. "Add more thread," he says, grabbing the skeins of green and yellow. "Make this work. I'm not missing out on your friendship because of a sizing error." He knots some more thread to the end of my bracelet to make it longer, which totally distracts from the expert workmanship and perfect arrow design, and holds out his arm for me to tie it on.

"There," I say as I tighten the knot, "it's official. Now we can be friends."

"And that's how you do it, folks." Jay holds his arm up to the camera, which I had now completely forgotten about. "That's how you can use a friendship bracelet to make a new friend. Thanks, Andi."

Scrambling, I quickly grab my forgotten camera and try to turn it off. All of that was filmed—Jay ribbing me, my confession about my dad, and that shameless flirting. My hands fumble the camera as I poke at the power button, and it slips into my lap. I grab it before it crashes to the floor, but my hand continues to shake as I remember everything Jay and I said to each other that was captured on film.

"Now you forgot about the camera, huh?" he says.

"No," I lie.

Jay narrows his eyes at me and laughs. "Well, don't worry about it. It's not like you can use that footage, anyway."

"You don't want me to put your confession online? Don't worry, Jay. I don't have that many followers anyway."

"I guess you can blackmail me if you want to."

"Well, you're lucky I'm not evil."

"Yup. I am lucky." He smiles down at the bracelet on his arm and then up at me. "So, do you want to go back out there, or do you want to craft some more?"

A quick glance at my festival app shows I have about

an hour until Tarot Card takes the stage, so I hop up from my chair. "Let's go."

After I wave to Patrick, who barely looks up from his phone, and the Cs, who are still working on those boxes, I slip the pink and purple diamond design bracelet, the first one I did, into my back pocket and run my fingers over the lumpy, crooked black, white, and gray bracelet Jay just gave me. I listened as he talked about all the disgusting pranks he plays in his videos and he explained it all and then I accepted this bracelet and his friendship. Part of me feels like a hypocrite—I hate everything he stands for, every stupid second of every stupid video on his stupid channel, even if it is all just an act. But another part of me knows that it's okay to change your mind about things when you get new information, especially when that new information tells you that you aren't so different after all. And still another part of me feels all scrambled up by that face. That smile. That shock of electricity when he looks at me.

I don't know what the right thing is. All I know is that I so desperately want to believe he is a good person in real life.

Once we get outside, we only walk a few feet before Jay stops abruptly and turns to face me. "There's actually something else I wanted to ask you," he says, taking a step and then another. He's so close I can feel his body humming against mine. Part of me wants to take two steps back, to reclaim the normal, friendly space between us, and part of me wants to climb him like monkey up a tree.

He reaches out his hand and grabs my fingers, squeezing lightly. "I really want to kiss you right now. I mean, not just right now. I wanted to kiss you the second I met you. But the more I talk to you, the more I want to kiss you. And I've kind of gotten to the point where I can hardly think of anything else. But I don't want it to be a disaster. I don't want this to be one of those things you look back on as an awful thing that happened on this day. So, is it okay if I kiss you right now? Or is that a bad idea?"

I wrap my arms around his waist, and I pull him a tiny bit closer. Now I actually can feel his body against mine, and it's solid, and the contact makes me shiver, even in this heat.

He moves his face slightly closer to my face, but not all the way. It's a delicious distance between the two of us. He's so close, I can feel the tickle of his breath on my face, and now my arms squeeze closer. All I would need to do to close the distance between us is rise up on my toes to meet him.

"You are killing me, Andi," he says. "Can you please let me know if it is okay for me to kiss you right now?" Our eyes are locked, and he looks as desperate as I feel.

"Thank you for asking," I say, breathy. "That was pretty sexy." And before I can think about it, or overthink about it, I let my body make the decision for me. "Yes, please. Kiss me now."

The words are barely out before his mouth is on mine. His hands move up to my cheeks, and his lips are soft and sweet and slow. At first. I kiss him back, and I guess he gets the impression that I am happy about this situation, because he says, "Mmmm," right into my mouth and kisses me again.

He slides his hands from my cheeks back to my neck, which makes me lean my head into his hand. He kisses his way over to my ear, where he whispers, "God, I've wanted to do this all day." Then he kisses my ear, which makes my entire body shiver.

And just like that his lips are back on mine. But he's not soft and slow anymore. He pulls me closer and I pull him closer and his tongue is in my mouth and my tongue is in his mouth, and kissing has never, ever felt like this before. It has never turned me inside out and given me chills and made me feel like I'm on fire at the same time. It has never made me feel like I was in another world entirely.

I don't know how long we exist in that other world, that world of Jay and his hands and his mouth and his body pressed against mine. I know that we don't stop kissing. I know that my hand moves from his neck, back to his hair, and finally moves down his arm where it grabs on to his delicious biceps and refuses to let go.

I know that his hand follows a similar pattern, but instead of ending on my arm, it has crawled the slightest bit up under my shirt on my back, so it touches my bare skin, and somewhere in the back of my mind I'm considering getting a tattoo of his hand there so I never forget this moment right now.

I know that he seems to enjoy taking his tongue and running it along my bottom lip every now and then, and I can't even really describe how it leaves me completely undone.

I know that in return I lightly bite his bottom lip and it elicits this noise from him, it comes from somewhere in the back of his throat, and it is the sexiest sound I have ever heard.

And I know that kissing Jay Bankar feels like the rightest thing that has ever happened to me in my entire life.

At one point in our kissing, some people walk by us, talking loudly about something or other, and their voices remind me we are outside in the middle of a music festival surrounded by thousands of people, and, even though the darkness is creeping in, we're still in public. I slowly pull away from Jay, even though I don't really want to.

"So, um . . ." What even am I trying to say? My brain hasn't snapped back into reality quite yet. I'm still spinning.

He laughs softly. "Yeah. I don't . . ."

I lean forward and kiss him again, quickly and softly, and then I squeeze his fingers.

"So, uh, friendship?" he says, leaning over so his forehead rests on mine.

I smile as I play with his fingers, running my thumb over the tips of each one. "I'm not sure," I say. "Is this how friends behave?"

He grabs my restless hand and laces our fingers together. I squeeze, and he squeezes back. "I think we need some more time to figure that out."

"But maybe not right in the middle of traffic?"

He pulls our hands up to his mouth and kisses my hand. "Yeah, that's probably a good call. We're kinda like zoo animals right here."

Hand in hand, we walk into the Main Stage crowd until we find an empty spot to sit. Every single nerve ending in my body is on high alert, yelling *I just kissed Jay Bankar!* so loudly that I can hardly process anything else, like what band is playing or anything going on around us. Jay said he wanted to kiss me since the moment we met, and, if I'm being completely honest with myself, I have wanted the same thing. I just didn't dare let myself think about it. But now that it happened, I'm having a hard time remembering what Past Andi's problem even was.

We still have some time before meeting up with Jordan, so I enjoy every second of being alone with Jay. We hold hands and snuggle close to each other and then he puts his arm around me, and I lean my head on his shoulder. My head on his shoulder means my nose is close to his neck, and with every one of my inhales, I smell him. It was hot all day, so his skin smells a little like sweat. But he also has this guy smell. Whatever combo of gum and man deodorant and cologne and laundry detergent he uses has made this delicious smell that I inhale with every breath. I'm trying to pay attention to the band, whoever they are, I really am, but his sexy man smell is too overwhelming, and I end up giving in to it, leaning up to kiss him while the music vibrates around us.

After a few songs from the band I'm not even paying attention to, I start to shiver, goose bumps popping up all over my arms, and it takes me a minute to realize that it's because the sun has almost completely set and the nighttime desert chill has crept in, not just because of my proximity to Jay and my memory of that kiss, playing on repeat in my mind.

"I think I need to run back to the tent and change," I say, breaking the spell between us. "These shorts aren't going to cut it much longer."

"Good call," Jay says. "I could definitely use a hoodie." He stands up and reaches his hand out to me. I take it, and he pulls me to my feet, then yanks me into him, so our bodies are pressed together. This closeness brings me back to the first night and our hug, before I knew who he was, and I'm reminded of how perfectly our bodies fit together. He lets go of my hand and wraps his arms around my waist, clasping his hands together and pulling me closer. "Let's head out now so we can make it back for Tarot Card."

I stand up as tall as I can on my toes and plant a kiss right on his lips. "Or not," I say playfully.

Jay smiles, and I know he picked up on my meaning. Maybe we'll go out to the tent to change and come right back for one of my favorite bands, but if we get stuck at the tent, well, would that be such a bad thing? "Is your brother still with Sadie?"

"He must be, because he said he would text me if he went anywhere." I look up at Jay and raise my eyebrows. "Let's go."

CHAPTER 9

›› • ‹‹

JAY AND I WALK BACK TO THE CAMPSITE, HAND IN hand, grinning at each other like fools. Yes, we do need to change into warmer clothes for the night, but I'm also hoping we can take advantage of the small shred of privacy we can get on these festival grounds for just a little bit. And from the way he keeps squeezing my hand, he seems to be hoping the same thing.

I'd hate to miss Tarot Card, but I can't deny there's a pull in Jay's kiss, in his body. I have to follow that pull and see where it leads. I mean, I can always catch a video of Tarot Card's set, but there will be no do-overs of this moment.

Like a good sister, I text Jordan to see where he is. He texts back that he's introducing Sadie to the dulcet tones of Horror Street and the deliciousness of Spice Pie, so I don't even need to tell him not to come back to the campsite quite yet. I just tell him I'm with Jay and not to worry, and I slip my phone back in my pocket.

The two of us turn the corner onto our little campsite

street, and my skin buzzes with anticipation. I practically skip up to my tent because I don't have anything else to do with all the adrenaline building up inside of me. Where is this night going to take us?

"Warm clothes and meet back here in five?" I say to Jay, smiling.

"Sounds like a plan," he says, returning my smile with a sly one of his own. But instead of turning toward his campsite, he pulls me in to him, pressing our bodies tight. He wraps his arms around me and leans into me and then we're kissing. A kiss that starts off sweet and gentle, but as Jay's hand travels up the back of my head, his fingers sliding through my hair, things quickly turn deeper. More intense.

I'm about to try to slip my hand under Jay's T-shirt and run my fingers along the skin of his back when I hear literally the last thing on earth I want to hear.

Dev Bankar's voice. The biggest ladyboner killer ever.

"Jay. What are you doing." It's not a question.

We jump apart, and the sly smile on Jay's face is immediately replaced with confusion and conflict. "Oh," he says. "Andi was just, uh, going to show me, uh, get me something."

In a matter of seconds, Jay completely changes. Morphs from the confident, charming guy he was with me earlier into this scared, submissive kid. I hardly recognize him in the shadow of his brother.

Dev looks at me. No, he turns his head in my direction, but he looks through me. He takes a long drag of his cigarette, then he blows out a trail of smoke. "Well, hurry up," he says. "I've been texting you. We have stuff to do."

Jay crosses his arms. "You said you'd leave me alone tonight." He sounds like a frightened child talking to his disciplinarian parent, not like an eighteen-year-old adult. "You promised."

"Well, things changed. Now hurry." He tosses his cigarette on the ground and steps on it. "We need to talk."

"But Tarot Card is on soon," Jay says, lifting his hand toward the direction of the festival I'm not sure we had any intention of returning to this evening. "You know—"

"Jay. I'm over this. Get what you need and get over here." He turns and disappears into their elaborate campsite space, leaving Jay looking frustrated and me with my mouth hanging open.

"Well, screw that," I say. But I can tell already that the mood has been killed and that our plans for some making out have been completely ruined, thanks to Dev and his cockblocking, wet-blanket, jerk-off attitude.

"I'm sorry, Andi." Jay steps close to me, but there's no chemistry in our closeness now.

"Wait. Are you listening to him? Are you leaving?"

"I have to."

"Why?" I cross my arms. "Because he said so? That's bullshit. You don't have to do everything he says."

"It's not that, it's just that—"

"That what? That you willingly do what your asshole brother says, no matter what? No matter how awful it is? No matter if it's directly opposite of what you really want to do?"

"No, that's not what—"

"So then you're telling me that leaving right now, going over there with him, that's what you *want* to do?"

He shakes his head, looking entirely defeated. "You know that's not it."

"No," I say, lowering my voice. "I really don't. Because all I see is you standing here in front of me, looking me in the face, and making that choice."

I struggle to keep my anger under control because I don't want Dev to hear me. But it's more than anger pulsing through me right now, it's embarrassment. I'm mortified I let Jay kiss me like that and I believed in that chemistry and now this is happening.

It might not have been captured on camera, but he totally pranked me.

He steps closer again, but this time I back up. He reaches for my hand, but I pull it away.

"Andi, please," he says. "Please try to understand. I told you about my brother. I told you how things are between us."

"You didn't tell me that he makes all of your decisions for you. No wonder he's such a jerk. You enable him."

"It's not like that."

"Prove it." I step closer now, and I bring my hands up his arms and wrap them around his neck. I step up on my toes and lean up to his ear and whisper, "Stay." I gently kiss his neck, and the rush of chemistry slams back into me at full force. "Stay with me for a little while."

He shivers under the touch of my tongue on his ear. He turns his head toward his campsite, and then turns back to me. "Just a few minutes?"

"Is that all you want? Just a few minutes?" I'm kissing down the side of his face now, softly and slowly, down to his neck.

"Ugh," he says. "Screw him."

Victorious, I smile and pull Jay into my tent by his hand. It's a total mess in here, but it's dark, and there's no way he really cares, so I shove my stray clothes under the pillow and hope for the best.

He joins me on my air mattress, but before anything happens, he pulls out his phone. "I'm just telling him to chill," he says. "And that I'll be back later."

Who knows what later means in Jay time, but I decide not to dwell on it and enjoy the fact that, for now, I won. I won this battle, and Jay and I are alone together. Finally.

"Now," he says, tossing his phone to the side. "Where were we?" He leans over and kisses me softly. I wrap my arm around his neck, and I pull him closer, so close that I can hardly tell where I end and he starts.

"I don't think we were quite here," I say. "But it's a good place to start." We kiss for a minute or two, but then his phone makes a noise.

"Ugh." He lets out an annoyed groan. "Sorry."

We keep kissing, but it makes a noise again. He sits up. "Let me just . . . ," he says, feeling around in the dark for his phone.

As he's looking at it, I say, "Can't you turn it off?"

He types something on the phone, then he puts it down. "Sorry," he says. He leans back into me, and we're at it again. I'm distracted at first, by the phone and by Dev and by Jay's reaction outside. But then, after a minute or two, that chemistry takes over. It's undeniable, this thing between us. And even when I'm frustrated with him, it burns under my skin. I grip his shoulders tightly and pull him even closer.

His fingers have been grazing the skin on my back between the waistband of my shorts and my tank top. His hand flattens there, fingers sliding under my shirt. "Is this okay?" he asks into my mouth.

"Mmm-hmm," I manage. His fingers, his hands on my bare skin . . . that's all so much more than okay.

His hand slides up my back, and I'm caught somewhere between trying not to explode and trying to figure out if I should do the same to him, when the loud *ziiiippp* of the zipper breaks through my thoughts.

"Hold on," I hear Jordan saying, and before I have a

chance to sit up or get some space between me and Jay or fix my shirt, which has kinda ridden up, my brother's head is inside our tent.

"Aaah!" I scream.

"Oh, shit," Jay says.

"Nooooo," Jordan moans, and crawls back out of the tent.

I yank my shirt down, and I climb over Jay and out to find my brother, who stands there with a very embarrassed-looking Sadie.

"What are you doing?"

"You didn't tell me you were here," he says. "I didn't know."

"You said you were watching Horror Street. I didn't think I had to."

Jay crawls out of the tent now, his hat on backward and his hair sticking out the front of it.

"Oh, hey," he says. "Uh, sorry about that."

"Don't apologize," I say. "He's the one who just barged in." I look at Sadie, who seems like she's trying to melt into the ground. "Sorry, Sadie."

"Oh, um," she mumbles. "It's . . . um."

"No, it's okay," Jay says. "I should probably get going anyway."

"What? No." I grab his hand. "You can't leave now."

He pulls me close. "I'm sorry," he whispers in my ear. "I really need to."

God, I hate Jordan. This is his fault. Jay chose me, and things were going so well. All of the outside issues—Dev, Dad, money, this day—had washed away, and it was just me and Jay and this connection between us. And then my brother had to come push it all off the ledge where it had been very carefully balancing.

"Actually," Sadie says, "I should probably go, too."

"What? No." Jordan says the exact same thing as me, and he grabs Sadie's hand. "Don't leave. It's not a big deal." He pulls her close and talks into her ear, saying whatever smooth Jordan things he can think of to get her to stay. But I can see leaving all over her face.

I turn from them and look up at Jay, who also has leaving all over his face.

"This isn't about you, okay? I promise. You're amazing." He kisses my cheek. "You're unbelievable."

I don't say anything, because what is there to say?

"Let me take care of this thing with my brother, okay? I'll talk to him, and we can spend the whole day together tomorrow."

"After the scavenger hunt," I say.

"Yeah," he says. "After the scavenger hunt." He lets out a long sigh. "Which my brother has ruined for me, by the way. I don't even want to do it tomorrow."

"Perfect," I say with a smile. "Drop out and then I can win. Done."

"If only it was that easy." He leans over and kisses

me softly on the mouth. "I promise we'll pick back up tomorrow, okay?"

"Okay." I'm sad and disappointed, but maybe this is all for the best right now. I could probably use the time away from Jay to process all of this. "See you tomorrow?"

"Without a doubt." He kisses me one more time, and I'm tempted to pull him closer and kiss him more intensely, but I'm reminded my brother is next to us when Jordan clears his throat.

Jay holds his wrist up and points at the friendship bracelet I made him, secured tightly to his arm, then he says goodbye to all of us and walks into his campsite compound.

By this time, Jordan has also said good night to Sadie, who said she was tired and just wanted to get back to her tent. Jordan and I shake our heads at each other.

"Sorry," Jordan says.

I shrug. "I didn't tell you. I'm sorry I yelled."

Now it's his turn to shrug. "This is the perfect ending to a perfect day, isn't it?"

"Dad let it get a little better this year, but I guess he drew the line at letting either of us hook up."

"Yeah, Dad doesn't want to see that."

"Can you blame him?"

He plops down on one of the folding chairs next to the tent. "So, what now?"

"Well, Tarot Card is on the Outdoor Stage in, like, ten minutes. We can still make it back there."

"Let's do it," he says.

We both quickly change into our jeans and hoodies and then head back out to the festival to catch Tarot Card and the last few bands of the evening. Jordan throws his arm around me, and I lean into my brother's familiar shoulder.

"This year was easier," he says.

I nod. "It still sucked, but it wasn't quite as bad."

"I guess it will get a little less bad every year, huh?"

"Part of me wants to say I hope so, but part of me doesn't," I say. "Is that weird?"

"Nah," he says. "I know exactly what you mean."

We walk like this, me leaning into his arm wrapped around me, all the way back to the festival. I spend the rest of the night jumping back and forth between memories of Dad and decisions about Jay and wondering what advice my father would have for me if he were here.

CHAPTER 10

>>> • <<<

I MANAGE TO GET A DECENT NIGHT'S SLEEP DESPITE the drone of terrible screamo music from next door and my mind running over and over and over my night with Jay. Saturday wore me out, so I guess the reinflated air mattress and both earplugs were all I really needed to drown it all out. As I hit yoga then wait in the shower line, my emotions don't know which way is up. On one hand, I'm looking forward to today. The very real possibility of winning and earning this interview has turned me into a bundle of nerves and frenetic energy. I mean, meeting and interviewing the band? Literally changing my life? It's all too much, and I shift from foot to foot and swing my shower basket back and forth as I wait in the shower line, almost hitting the girl in front of me in the back of the knees at least twice.

But then there's Jay, who also has me feeling apprehensive, and so does the fact that it's the last day of the festival. I've really gotten used to sleeping on an air mattress and showering in my flip-flops, and after this I'm going back home to school and my same old same old, which definitely doesn't include this much live music or hot guy interaction.

The shower line moves faster today; I guess most people have given up on showering by the last day of the festival. To be completely honest, if I hadn't met Jay right when I got here, I might have given up on it myself. No real need to worry about being clean when everyone around you is covered in a layer of funk.

I find myself actually skipping back to the campsite after my shower. Part of me wants to peek behind the Bankar curtain and see what Jay is up to, but I don't want to poke the grumpy bear that is Dev. I'll wait until the final scavenger hunt task.

Instead, I wake Jordan up and cook some breakfast. As we eat, we discuss our master plan. We could either leave tonight after the Known are done with their headlining set, driving back home tired and in the dark. Or we could sleep here at the campsite after the last band and leave in the morning, school be damned. I'm Team Good Night's Sleep and Jordan is Team Drive Home Exhausted, for reasons I can't really fathom. We compromise by tearing down as much of the campsite as we don't need and packing it in the car, so if we do decide to leave, we can pull down the tent and hop on the road, but if we decide to stay, we can just flop down onto our air mattresses.

By the time we have the car packed as much as we can, it's time to meet Hipster Matthew, so we head in to the festival.

"I hate to bring this up," Jordan says as we scan our wristbands, "since this morning is going so smoothly so far, but it's our last day here, and—"

I hold up my hand to stop him. "I know what you're going to say."

"Do you, now?"

"You're going to say that it's our last day here and I still have nothing for a Cabazon video aside from festival background footage and boring interviews with randoms."

Mom has been texting, asking for status updates. I don't want to lie to her, but I also don't want to tell her that I have completely failed. That I have nothing. So I reply to all of her texts with a bunch of emojis instead of an actual answer.

But I have no choice but to face Jordan, who is right here next to me and not on the other end of a phone. Somewhere in the back of my mind is a little voice telling me that I need to accept the fact that there is a good chance I'm not winning this interview with the Known today, that I'm not going to come up with any other brilliant idea, and that I'm going to leave this festival exactly the way I came—with no way to afford SCU next year. I've been trying to ignore that voice, but the damn thing has been getting louder every day, and at this point it's practically screaming at me.

Since I can't answer my brother with a bunch of emojis, I just say, "I'll figure something out," my voice dripping with a confidence I don't actually possess. "Don't you worry about me."

"I would never worry about you getting something done." He smiles as he gently hip-checks me. "I was just thinking that if you don't—"

"Don't even put that out in the universe, Jordan. I'm going to figure something out."

"Okay," he says, his voice quiet. "Okay."

It's not often that things get awkward between me and my twin brother, but that's the only way I can describe the vibe that settles over us.

"I'm really going to miss Hipster Matthew," I say, in a desperate attempt to get things back on track.

"I'm going to miss his fedora," Jordan says, and I'm relieved he's playing along.

"I'm going to miss these random pieces of art," I say, waving my hand at a tree with a variety of body parts—hands, feet, bones—hanging from it.

"I'm going to miss Spice Pie."

"Mmm. Spice Pie."

"Do we have time for Spice Pie right now?"

I smack him. "Dude, we just ate breakfast."

"Like, two hours ago."

"Well, we don't have time. We'll treat ourselves to Spice Pie after we win this scavenger hunt."

The way that things shook out over the past two days, Jay and I are in a tie, so today is critical. Sadie is right behind us, but I'm not too worried about her. And I'm especially not worried about Quan and the Cs, who technically could come from behind in a major upset but just don't seem to share my competitive spirit. Or just aren't as desperate.

So right now with Jay I'm out for blood. Then, after I win and this is over, we can go back to what we had going on last night.

When we get to the meeting spot, Hipster Matthew is chatting with Cody and Corey, who are sporting matching the Known concert tees today, and we hop into the conversation until Quan and Sadie show up. Finally Jay arrives, and right off the bat, two weird things sound the alarm bells. Number one, he's visibly flustered. His cheeks are red, his hair is a mess, and he looks unkempt.

The second odd thing is that he's alone. No Dev.

Despite the super weird feeling his arrival gives me, I smile at Jay and try to give him a knowing look, a look that hopefully says I can't wait for this to be over so we can hang out and be normal. But instead of returning the look, or giving me a smile or a wink or a nod or a hand gesture or anything, he pretends like he doesn't even see me. He directs his gaze to the grass under his flip-flops like he's waiting for it to do tricks.

I want to ask him if everything is okay or where his brother is, but he's obviously intent on ignoring me. Maybe he needs to get into intense game mode for this last leg of the scavenger hunt. It seems Dev is the competitive one out of the two, so if he isn't even here, I don't see what the big deal is.

At least he's wearing his bracelet, I think as I absently play with the stringy ends of the one he made for me, still tied around my wrist.

Jordan leans in to me. "What's up with your boy?"

"No clue." I'm glad Jordan notices this weirdness, this offness in Jay, too, and it's not simply me being paranoid.

Hipster Matthew, wearing a branded tank top today and showing off his farmer-tanned arms, holds up his camera and launches in on his rehearsed speech. "Mobilocity and I are so excited for our last day of the Cabazon Scavenger Hunt. We hope you've had as much fun as we have." I try to listen to him, but I can't stop watching Jay out of the corner of my eye. He still hasn't looked up, and now his arms are crossed in front of him in the textbook definition of negative body language. Something is up.

"Today's final task is a little more complicated. Not only will you have to find things to photograph, but you'll also need to find festivalgoers to be in the photos with you. It should be a fun opportunity to meet some new people and explore some sides of the festival you haven't seen yet." My ears perk up at "meet some new people." This sounds right up my alley.

"Anyone need a charge? I'm going to head over to the charging station to get your clues and your loaner phones." Matthew collects the phones and battery packs we want him to charge; he is the only reason I've had a charged phone battery all weekend. I'll be really glad to get back to civilization again, where I won't have to pass my phone off to a bearded stranger on the daily just to keep it from dying.

"Be back in a few," he says and retreats to the charging station, leaving me alone with Jay and his weirdness.

"Should I try to talk to him?" I ask Jordan.

"Well, I'm going to go talk to Sadie, so it's either talk to him or stand here by yourself."

I smack him on the arm, and I walk over to Jay, whose arms are still crossed. He might as well be wearing a sandwich board that says STAY AWAY, and something in the back of my mind tells me I really should listen.

"Hey," I say. "You all right?"

"Yeah, I'm fine. Why?" There's nothing kind in his voice, and I recognize it immediately. It's his video voice. His asshole voice.

"Jay. What's going on?"

"Don't take this the wrong way," he says, "but I really don't want to talk to you right now."

I stare at him for a second, really take in his face. No longer flustered, now his features are hardened. There's hardly anything in him that reminds me of the Jay I've spent time with over the past few days.

His eyes, though. His eyes are desperate. Pleading.

I wait for a couple of seconds, give him a chance to say whatever it is his eyes are trying to ask, but he doesn't.

"Fine," I say, shoving my hands into the back pockets of my shorts and turning around. "I won't make you."

He starts to say something; I hear sounds coming out of his mouth. But he seems to change his mind, and as I walk away, the sounds float off into the air before ever forming into words.

Unbelievable. After everything he shared with me yesterday. After our long conversation and everything he told me about his brother, he's acting like this. I got played, exactly like I knew I was going to when I first realized who he was.

And yet I shouldn't even be surprised. That's the worst part of all of this. I called it right away, I knew it was inevitable, and then I let myself get caught up in it, in him, in the heady rush of feelings, anyway.

Jordan is talking to Sadie, so I join them as quickly as I can to get away from Jay, like I should have as soon as we met.

"Hey, Andi," Sadie says as I approach. I raise a hand in greeting, but I don't trust myself to say anything. My voice will give it all away. The hurt, the betrayal.

But who needs words when you have a twin? All it takes is one look at my face, and Jordan says, "Oh, shit. Uh, Sadie. Can you give us a sec?"

She nods, and Jordan pulls me away from the crowd of scavenger hunters. "Spill," he says. "What happened?"

I shake my head. Explaining what went down between me and Jay is impossible because it was so much more than what was said.

"He was . . ." I wave my hand around, as if I can summon up the words I need to explain what all that was. "He was the guy from the videos. Not his normal self, his fake self. His jerk self. I don't know why he's doing this act right now, but I thought we were past this."

Jordan scratches his head as he looks off into the distance, like he's trying to come up with something to say. "Look," he says finally. "I'm not trying to be a dick here, but are you surprised? I mean, you knew who he was."

I shake my head again. I haven't told Jordan too much about my conversation with Jay last night, about his life with his brother and their serious money issues. I want to say, *But he told me that wasn't him*, but those words sound so ridiculous, even to me. It's too late to try to explain now. It'll just come off like I'm trying to convince myself, which I guess is exactly what is happening.

My brother pulls me into a hug and part of me wants to pull away because I don't want Jay to see what he's done to me. But I need the comfort from Jordan. And I also want Jay to see that what he does, the way he acts, hurts people. I can't believe he doesn't care about that at all.

"Can you get this off of me, please?" I hold my wrist out to my brother, trying to keep my arm from shaking with anger. Jordan struggles with the knot.

"It's too tight. We'll cut it off later, okay?"

"Okay, everyone. Are you ready for some fun?" Hipster Matthew has returned, and he carries with him today's clues.

Now, in the mood I'm in, I don't even feel like doing any of this. I want to drown my sorrows in a slice of Spice Pie, an enormous Coke, and the loudest band I can find. Music. That's what will cure me.

But then I remember why I'm here, and it's sure as hell not for Jay. I need this interview for my channel. This is me going to college. This is me staying with my brother. This is me following in my dad's footsteps.

This is my future.

"We have to kick his ass now," Jordan whispers in my ear again, and I know he's right. On top of all my personal reasons, I need to win for the pride.

There's no way this asshole is going to beat me.

"Here we go, everyone!" Hipster Matthew holds up

his camera in one hand and the clues in the other. "It's still anyone's game. So, let's have fun out there today. Remember, an exclusive interview with the Known is at stake." He distributes the clues, and then, with a flourish, announces, "And, GO!"

I flip over our clue. Like Friday's bingo card, this one has a list of pictures around the festival to take. FIND SIX, it says at the top, and a list follows.

Band/artist that would never play Cabazon
Celebrity lookalike
White boy wasted
Mobilocity in the wild
Animal
Festival fashion icon
Reading a book (yes, an actual book)
Real life Snapchat filter
Identical twins
Superfan

This is a random list, and I'm not even sure how to interpret some of them, but I'm not about to spend a second being negative. "Where should we start?"

"Beer garden," Jordan says. "White boy wasted times a million over there."

And we're off, running through the festival with a purpose. Yesterday I had been distracted by thoughts of Jay that threw me off my game, but today those thoughts fuel me to run faster. Now losing is not an option. I have to win. For the prize and the interview, sure, but more because Jay Bankar has to go down, and I have to be the person who does it.

"There." I point at a shirtless guy with a backward visor, which . . . what? He's gripping a plastic cup of beer in one hand and doing some off-beat arm choreography with the other one, and he looks like he would topple over with a strong breeze.

I trot up to the half fence surrounding the beer garden. "Hey! Visor guy! Come here!"

The guy wipes his sweaty forehead with the back of the hand that holds his beer and stumble-dances over to meet us.

"Hi, I'm Andi, and this is my brother, Jordan. What's your name?"

He gives us a head nod. "You can call me Butters."

"Hey, Butters. We're doing a scavenger hunt for Mobilocity to try to win an interview with the Known, and we're looking for the drunkest guy at the festival. Mind if we take a pic with you and post it for the contest?"

"Hell, yeah," Butters says. "I love the Known." He leans over the chain link to pose with me, holding his beer aloft with one hand and making devil horns with the other.

"Make sure you tag me!" he yells as we turn away to post the photo.

But it's not that easy. "There's nothing on this phone," Jordan says, shooting me a desperate look. "All the apps are gone. It's wiped."

"What?" I grab the loaner phone.

I poke at the screen as if that's all it will take to make everything that has been on this phone for the past two days appear, but it's obviously very ineffective. Jordan's right. This phone has a phone app, a camera, a clock, and the icon for the app store. And nothing else.

"We'll have to redownload everything," I whine. But when I click on the app store, a window requiring a password pops up. "Oh my God, it needs a password. I don't have a password."

"Try Mobilocity," Jordan says.

"Doesn't work." All the force in my body is going into my finger as I try different potential passwords to open the app store, but all my attempts are unsuccessful.

"Smashing the phone with your finger definitely won't help the situation," Jordan says. His voice sounds like he's somewhere between hysterical laughter and rage, and his comment puts me there, too.

"I'm just pretending it's Jay's face. And Dev's face. And Quan's face, while I'm at it, because I bet he and his millions of followers didn't get handed a wiped phone."

Finally, out of desperation, I try #MobilocityFamily, and it actually works. We're still connected to the secure Wi-Fi, so we're able to get everything set up much more quickly than if we had to rely on our network connection, but still, we lost a significant amount of time, and now both of us are ready to burn it all down.

Yesterday, we lost to Jay and Dev by less than a minute. Now we've spent almost five times that standing helplessly while we messed with this stupid phone. I'd give anything to be able to hit something right now, like a punching bag shaped like Jay's face. Or even Jay's actual face.

But, pissed or not, it's time to power through our list and try to make up those lost minutes. Normally, if given a task that involves meeting people, I'd be chatting up every person we encounter. Listening to their stories, finding out their favorite bands, hearing how their weekend was going. In fact, I'd probably spend so long getting everyone's life story that we'd lose the challenge by a landslide. But I'm sour on stories this weekend. I couldn't get a decent interview to save my life. And I actually listened to Jay's story, and look where that got me. People's stories are letting me down.

So even though this challenge should be fun, it's not. I go through the motions, determined to talk to each person as little as possible, worried less about enjoying myself and more—only—about making up our wasted time and winning.

We find Sasha, a pretty Black girl with long braids and flawless skin, wearing a flower crown dancing toward the back of the rave at the Palm Tree stage—real life Snapchat filter, check.

We almost trip over Noor, a small girl in a hijab sitting on a blanket, headphones in, probably drowning out the sound of the band playing at the Outdoor Stage, staring intently at a paperback copy of *Between the World and Me*—reading an actual book, check.

Snapping selfies under the gazebo Jay and I walked through yesterday is Janice, a tall, thin Asian girl wearing Doc Martens and a hot pink pleather bikini top with a tiny matching skirt—festival fashion icon, check.

Waiting in line at the kebab stand is JT, the whitest guy in America, wearing a Florida Georgia Line T-shirt and cowboy hat. JT must be lost; the country music festival is here at the polo grounds next weekend, but I don't bother telling him about it—band who would never play at this festival, check.

After we snap a quick photo with a girl named Lourdes who is wearing, by choice, Hipster Matthew's fake-vintage Mobilocity T-shirt, Jordan runs his finger down at the list. "That's six. We're done."

Then there's nothing to do but run.

CHAPTER 11

›› • ‹‹

"I THINK WE HAVE THIS," I SAY, SPRINTING BACK TO the meeting spot and probably knocking some innocent bystanders over on my way. I played soccer for years, and Jordan has always played basketball, so we're good runners, even though his legs are twice as long as mine. If this comes down to a footrace, we can totally compete. "Come on. We're almost there."

Hipster Matthew is right there; I can see his farmer's tan. He's playing on his phone and doesn't see us coming, which is awesome, because it means he's not even expecting a team to check in yet. Even with the time that was wasted with the stupid wiped phone, we are still in the lead. "We got this," Jordan yells.

And then, with the finish line less than fifty yards away and the end of this whole thing in sight, the Known so close I can smell their onstage sweat, my subscriber count already growing, and that tuition check to SCU being written, two skinny white guys about my age walk directly in front of me, throwing me off course.

"Oh, so sorry," they say loudly. "Our fault."

"Move it," I yell as I maneuver around them. But as I run to the side, I find a small group of Asian girls right in my path. "Out of the way," I say, but instead of clearing the way for me, they move farther into where I'm running, giggling as they seem to try to block me from getting by them. "What the hell?"

And then as I get through that gauntlet, I slam directly into a huge Latino guy in a Morrissey T-shirt. "Sorry," he says, but he takes a step back into my path as I try to take off again. With both of us moving in the same direction, and me trying to break back into a run, my feet tangle with his, and I topple over, crumpling into a heap on the soft grass and landing hard on my right ankle.

"Aaahhh," I call out. I try to get up and keep running, but I only take a few steps before I stumble to the ground again.

"What happened?" Jordan asks. By now, people around us have stopped to stare. Most cast sympathetic glances our way, but I hear some snickering and see some finger pointing out of the corner of my eye.

"Those people. That guy." I rub my leg, and when I pull my hand away, I can see my ankle is red and already looks swollen, and I have scrapes up and down my shin from the fall.

"What guy?" Jordan asks, looking around.

"I don't know. There was a guy. He was in my way." I try to stand again, and, as I do, I search the area around me for all the people who were up in my space, but they are nowhere to be found.

"Don't worry about it," I say. "Go." I try to run, but it's more of a hobble. I can't go as fast as I was before, pain shoots through my leg, and even though I'm pushing myself as hard as I can, I've slowed down considerably. I've fallen and twisted my ankle many times on the soccer field and still run just fine, but that was when I was all warmed up in the middle of a game, not trying to bust into a dead sprint. Running superfast with an injury is just not happening right now.

And then, out of nowhere from behind us, comes Jay. Running is no problem for him, and he easily passes us. Well, he passes *me*, anyway, but Jordan can't win without me. Jay hops onto the grass in front of Hipster Matthew and lets out a loud, primal yell followed by a victory dance of some sort. And while Jay is screaming and dancing, Dev appears holding a GoPro from behind a hippo sculpture and runs up to meet his brother.

The hippo sculpture is right near where I was running when all the random people started wandering directly in my path.

Jordan and I slow to a walk as Dev films his brother being congratulated with a side hug and a back slap from Matthew. Then he turns the camera on us as we approach.

"Aww, here they are. Team Loser," Dev says. I didn't think he was ever on these videos, but he is using this different, fake voice that happens to sound a lot like Jay's fake voice. He's impersonating Jay, trying to sound like him for this video, and it's working. Jay said his brother was too awkward to be on camera, but he certainly has the voice for the part. In fact, this fake voice sounds eerily similar to Jay's. I wonder how often some of the voice-overs on their channel are actually Dev and not Jay.

"You sent those people." I get right up in Dev's face, trying to avoid the camera he keeps repositioning to capture my reaction. "You had those people get in my way on purpose! That guy tripped me! You did that so you could win and film it."

I whirl around to face Hipster Matthew now. "Didn't you see that, Matthew? You were right there. Didn't you see those people interfering? Look, they tripped me. I hurt my ankle." I stick my scraped-up leg toward him as evidence.

Matthew looks like he wants to disappear, like he wants to crawl inside his beard and hide in it forever. He obviously doesn't know how to handle conflict that isn't in his scripted monologue.

Dev stays silent; he just keeps filming with a smirk.

That silence pisses off my brother, who leaps into action.

"What the hell?" he says. "Why are you sending people after my sister?" He is in Dev's face now, towering over the still-filming camera, and he pushes Dev hard on the shoulder. "Say something, you sack of shit. And turn off this fucking camera." He shoves Dev again, and this time Dev stumbles backward. But he's silent and he keeps on smirking, keeps on filming. "And you wiped our phone, too, didn't you? How did you manage that one?"

"Jordan, don't," I say, pulling him back. The last thing we need is a video of him starting a fight over some dumb scavenger hunt ending up online and jeopardizing his scholarship. "He's not worth it."

Then I turn to Jay, who stands there watching this all go down but doing nothing, saying nothing. He has an expression of vague horror on his face, his mouth hanging open slightly, but aside from that, he's unresponsive.

"And you," I say, narrowing my eyes at him. "You knew this was going to happen, didn't you? That's why you were so shady earlier." I'm tempted to trip him and kick his leg so he can see how it feels. "You are such a piece of shit. Everything you told me was a lie. Everything. This is what you came for, isn't it? To get a video like this? And you knew it would be me from the second we met."

He shakes his head, and his mouth closes, then opens again like he's going to respond. But then he looks at his brother, who has turned the camera on him, and his mouth snaps shut again. Silence.

"That was a violation of the rules, wasn't it, Matthew?" Dev says in that creepy fake-Jay voice. "You know I'm right."

"What rules?" Jordan and I snap at the same time.

"The 'no physical violence against any of the competitors' rule in the release we signed? I believe you just pushed me on the shoulder. That's physical violence, is it not? I think you need to be disqualified."

Hipster Matthew lets out a small sound of distress, and my mouth falls open. "You sent people to trip me, you asshole."

"I didn't touch you."

I turn to Jay again, just to see what he's doing after his brother has all but admitted to sending people to attack me, but he's staring at his phone like none of this even matters to him.

Cody and Corey choose this unfortunate moment to run up. They're wearing their normal carefree expressions, but as soon as they sense the tension, the easy smiles fall off their faces. "What's going on?" Cody asks.

"Uh . . ." Hipster Matthew says. He lost the reins on this situation so long ago, and now he struggles to regain some control. "Okay, Jay and Dev, you need to come with me right now. And everyone else, hang tight. If anyone else comes, uh, let them know we'll be right back."

I watch as Dev, who finally turned off his GoPro and

stuck it in his back pocket, walks off with Matthew. Jay trails behind them, walking slowly, head and shoulders slumped. He stops for a second and turns around. Our eyes meet and we stare at each other for a few long moments. His mouth turns down in a frown, and he mouths, *I'm so sorry*.

I narrow my eyes and shake my head. I'm not even going to dignify that BS with a response.

Jordan and I fill the Cs in on what happened, and while we tell them the story, Sadie and Quan finally show up. It doesn't take long before everyone is caught up on the Mobilocity scavenger hunt drama.

"I can't even believe that," Sadie says. "What a dick."

"And Jay didn't do anything?" Quan asks. "That's fucked up."

"He just stood there on his phone like he couldn't be bothered." I can't even believe the words as they come out of my mouth, and now that I've had time to process, the shock wears off and tears prick my eyes. I don't want to cry over Jay Bankar. I don't. Especially in front of all of these people. So I keep my tears inside, building up a flood of betrayal and disappointment. I close my eyes and pinch the bridge of my nose, sucking in and then letting out a few deep breaths to calm myself down. *He's not worth it, Andi*, I tell myself on my inhale, repeating what I said to Jordan earlier until I can make myself believe it. And with each exhale I imagine blowing him out of my life, like a huge gust of wind taking him somewhere far, far away.

As I breathe, a throb in my ankle reminds me why all of this is happening in the first place. I open my eyes and lean up to Jordan, whispering, "My leg is really killing me." I try to keep my voice steady and even, but my brother has seen and heard me at my highest high and lowest low. He knows I'm struggling.

"Let's see if there's a first aid tent," he mumbles. Then he says to the group, "Hey, we're going to take Andi to get her ankle checked out. Anyone know if there is first aid around here?"

"I'll go with you," Sadie offers.

"Oh, you don't need to do that," Jordan says, smiling. "But will you let Matthew know where we went? We still need to trade phones back with him."

Quan points us in the direction of an information booth, and from there we find the first aid tent, back by the main entrance. Inside it's cool and comfortable, and I'm so glad to sit down because the walk over here was more of a hobble.

"You okay?" Jordan asks while we wait.

"Are you talking about my ankle? Or are you talking about Jay?"

"Either," he says. "Both. All of the above."

I let out a long sigh. "I just can't believe that I knew

this was going to happen and I sat here and let it happen anyway." I lean my head on my brother's shoulder. "Why did I believe him even though all the evidence told me not to? Am I that gullible?"

"It's not that," he says. "You're an optimist. And you want to see the best in people. Even when that's not what they're showing off to the world. You seek out their good stuff. I don't think that's a bad thing."

"But I was wrong about the good stuff. I was totally wrong." The urge to cry pricks up again, but I fight it back by taking a few deep breaths. "I'm so tired of getting screwed over."

"Don't be dramatic," he says. "This is one time in your life you've been screwed over."

"No," I say, swinging my leg up on to Jordan's lap. "SCU."

"How is that getting screwed over? You got in. Yeah, it sucks that we can't afford it, and it sucks that you didn't get that scholarship, but it's not like there's some evil force working against you. You didn't make some error in judgment somewhere, and no one was out to get you." He smacks my knee lightly. "Shit just happened, like it does."

"This was all supposed to work out. It felt like destiny, you know? The Known, Dad's anniversary, an interview—it felt like a sign."

"This isn't over yet, Andi." Jordan pats my knee, gently this time. "There's still time for things to work out for you.

You didn't get an interview with the Known, but that doesn't mean your channel will never be successful. You didn't come up with some amazing idea for a video, but that's not the only way to make money. It doesn't mean that college is completely out of the picture."

"Maybe it's for the best, anyway." I lean my head back against the wall of the tent. "I like my channel the way it is."

We sit in silence for a minute, and then I let out a quick laugh. "You know what's funny? I've been telling myself I need to go to SCU so I can help you keep your life in order, but here you are keeping *my* life in order."

"You think I need your help to function? I'm not that helpless."

"I know you're not," I say, smiling up at my brother. "It's just going to be a lot for you. Basketball, school, all of it. I don't want you to mess it all up."

"Freaking *yikes*, Andi." He pushes my leg off his lap. "I don't need you to babysit me. I mean, I want you to come to SCU if that's what you want, but don't feel like you have to be my nanny or something. I'm not a child." There's a strong hint of annoyance in his voice, but before I get a chance to explain myself, my name is called, and I hobble over to the newly available exam table.

The first aid tent diagnoses me with a mild sprain. The hot medical volunteer doesn't mind that I film him for whatever video I decide to throw together as he wraps my ankle with an Ace bandage, and he sends me on my way with lots of extra-strength over-the-counter drugs to help with the pain and orders to take it easy for the rest of the night. The rest has helped it feel better already, so I'm able to walk pretty confidently back to meet with Hipster Matthew and get my phone back.

"Are you really going to put this on a video?" Jordan asks as we pass a hip-hop act on the Main Stage.

I shrug. "I have no idea. I think it depends on what happens right now. Do you think we'll actually get disqualified?"

"I hope not," he says. "And if we do, I'm sorry."

"Don't be." I put my hand on his arm. "I'm glad you stuck up for me like that. You're a good brother."

"I'm not going to stand there while some jackass sabotages you. I'm not a total dick."

We find Hipster Matthew waiting for us in the normal spot, and Sadie waiting with him. She waves and smiles when we approach.

"How are you feeling, Andi?" Hipster Matthew asks.

I kick out my leg to show off my neon pink bandage. "All wrapped up," I say. "Got some drugs. Feeling better now."

"Drugs from first aid and not some random tent in the campsite, I hope," he says, laughing.

"Matthew!" I cover my mouth in mock surprise. "I believe you just cracked an actual joke. I'm impressed."

He shakes his head, but he's smiling. He must know how ridiculous he is.

"Oh," he says. "Your phones. All charged." We take them and hand back our loaner phone. "So, my boss and I talked to Dev and Jay."

Just the mention of their names sends a shudder of revulsion through my body.

"Honestly, the whole situation looks pretty suspicious. But we have no proof Dev did anything to influence the outcome of the scavenger hunt, from wiping your phone to sending people to get in your way. And you didn't see him, right?"

"No, but I know—"

"I know," he says. "But if there isn't any proof, if no one saw anything, there's really nothing we can do. I'm sorry, Andi." He pats me awkwardly on my shoulder, the way a small child pats a dog before they learn how to pet.

"What about the rule about physical violence against another participant?" Jordan asks. "Are we disqualified from the whole thing?" Getting disqualified would mean giving up our prize from the first day and the cash we're supposed to win from coming in second overall.

"Well, I have good news about that." Hipster Matthew wipes his hands down the front of his shorts. "I checked with my boss, and since neither Jordan nor Dev were official participants, just you and Jay were the ones who were actually competing, the rules don't apply to you guys. You can go ahead and beat the shit out of that asshole for all I care."

"Matthew, that's another joke! You're on a roll right now."

"So," Hipster Matthew says, a little twinkle in his eye. "Here's your cash prize for coming in second overall." He pulls an envelope out of his back pocket and hands it to me. "We all know you should have won, and I'm sorry about the drama. I wish there was something I could do."

I take the envelope, which is nowhere near the amount of money I would have made from the ad revenue from an interview with the Known and would probably pay for, like, one book at SCU, and I shove it in my back pocket with a shrug. "No worries." Of course I'm upset I didn't win. I wanted that interview, and it would have been a game-changer for my channel, and for my future. But it does make me feel better that at least Hipster Matthew knows what assholes the Bankar brothers are, even if there isn't anything he can do about it. "And, hey, you kept my phone charged for me for three days out here. That makes this whole thing worth it."

Hipster Matthew laughs and shakes hands with both of us. "Enjoy the rest of the festival," he says. "You should check out Lola Paige later on the Cactus Stage. She's awesome."

He walks back off to plug himself in to the Mobilocity

charging station or whatever he does when he isn't running this contest, leaving us alone with Sadie.

Sadie's eyebrows crinkle. "So, what now?"

Jordan throws an arm around each of our shoulders. "Girls, I think what we need right now is some more Spice Pie."

Once we get our pizzas, we find an empty patch of grass to sit down and talk. We fill Sadie in on the happenings of the day, and I get more and more upset the more I tell her about it.

"What are you going to do?" she asks. "You can't just let them get away with it."

I shrug. "Revenge isn't my thing. They know they're assholes. They have to wake up every morning and look in the mirror and know they're trash. That's enough for me."

Sadie's mouth falls open. "How can you not want to get them back? To do something to get even? You're a saint, Andi. I'd be plotting revenge like you wouldn't believe. Those guys wouldn't be able to sleep at night for wondering when I'd be showing up to make their lives miserable."

"Damn, girl," Jordan says, looking at her with a mix of terror and desire. This is exactly his kind of crazy. He can't resist a girl who is just a little bit off the rails.

But revenge isn't for me. Everything Jay told me last night, about his brother and how he completely runs his life, keeps bubbling up in my mind. What happened today was completely about Dev. Jay was complicit, yes. He went along with it. He could have stood up for me, and he chose not to. That was his choice, but I'm not going to expend more of my own energy to make him feel bad about it, when he obviously hates his situation already. Nope, I'm just going to stop caring.

"Aside from throwing some major shade his way in my next video, which will be a shock to absolutely no one"—I stand up, crinkling up my pizza trash and tossing it in the bin—"nope. I'm not going to do anything. I'm done."

I scan the festival, the crowds of people milling about, the groups gathered at each of the stages, dancing and having fun, and suddenly my body is weighed down with exhaustion. I don't know if it's the lack of quality sleep catching up with me, or my injury hitting me, or the BS with Jay simply overwhelming me, but all I want to do is lie down in my tent and close my eyes for a minute.

"Actually," I say. "I think I'm going to go back to the campsite for a bit."

"What?" Jordan hops up and puts his hands out, as if he's going to stop me physically. "No. Why? You're going to miss Outburst. They go on in thirty minutes."

I let out a long sigh.

"I know, but . . . I need some time alone, okay?" I try to communicate with him with only a look, because I don't want to get into all my feelings in front of Sadie. "You and Sadie go see Outburst. Have fun. I'll meet back up with you in an hour or two, okay? I'll text you."

I can tell Jordan doesn't want to let me go, but he does.

"Get some rest," he says.

"I will. See you later, Sadie."

She lifts her hand in a wave, and I turn and walk back to the campsite. The crowd seems thicker today. Maybe there really are more people, or maybe my anxiety over the day's events is making everyone feel closer, but either way it seems like I can't even move a foot in any direction without some sweaty body pushing into me.

I'm so anxious to escape from everything that happened at the festival today and retreat into the solitude of my tent. The closer I get, the faster I try to walk, which isn't easy with my ankle, but I'm weaving through the mass of people on the walkways back to the campground as best I can, trying to leave everything about this day behind me for a little while.

But I can't leave everything behind, because as I hobble through the crowd, my phone lights up with an incoming call from Mom.

I want so badly to ignore it. Shove the phone down deep in my pocket with everything else that has happened today, this whole weekend, and pretend it doesn't exist. But the more my phone vibrates in my hand, the more I know I really need some comfort right now, and there's no one better at comforting me than Mom.

"You answered!" she says when I pick up. "I was expecting another sunglasses emoji and eight more hours of radio silence."

"Sorry, Mom." I'm tired of dodging drunk people, so I find a clear grassy area near the general store to sit and talk for a minute. "I've had a rough day."

"Do you want to talk about it?"

I do, so I tell her everything—about Jay and the scavenger hunt and his betrayal. I don't mention my injury, though, because I know she would freak the hell out, and I can't handle her trying to drive out here and kick Dev's ass right now.

"I told you I would come to this festival and make some incredible video that would make me go viral, but I couldn't think of anything. I had no plan, no big idea, and nothing ever came to me. It's so hard. I just want to keep doing what I was doing. That's what I like and what I'm good at. I don't care that it doesn't get me a million subscribers." I stretch my legs out in the grass, running my fingers through the long blades in an attempt to calm myself down. "I even tried to interview people like Dad did. I asked all the *Sam on the Streets* questions, but the people I found gave these boring answers, and it was all so dumb."

Mom laughs, a loud, sharp noise that almost causes me to drop the phone. "Oh, sweetie. I guess it's time for me to tell you a secret about your dad and *Sam on the Streets*."

"What?"

"It was scripted. All of the segments on his show were scripted."

"Those weren't real people?" Mom might as well have told me that Jordan isn't my brother, that's how earth-shattering this news is. My dad was famous for *Sam on the Streets*. The current morning show team on his station even does a knockoff version of it because so many listeners called in demanding that it live on. Their version pales in comparison, but that's what a huge deal Dad's show was.

"Sorry to have to be the one to tell you, but absolutely not. Do you think he got random people to talk about their long-lost loves by asking them about ice cream flavors? That everyone he ran into had some amazing story to tell? It was all set up, sweetie. Your dad and the morning show team wrote all of those segments, and most of the voices were from the interns and production staff. Even your dad would have gotten boring stories from people if he hadn't come up with the replies on his own. He was a radio DJ, not a journalist."

"So, the adopted baby . . ."

"Was completely scripted, yeah."

If I weren't already sitting, this admission would knock

me on my ass. But it does make me feel a little better about my complete inability to get a good response out of anyone yesterday using Dad's questions. Knowing that I don't suck at talking to people is my one tiny win on this craptastic day.

"Wow," I say, letting out a long breath. "Is *everything* I know about Dad a lie?"

"Of course not. But it's radio. It's entertainment. I'm not going to say that every single thing they did was scripted, but if it wasn't an interview with a band, then it was probably Large Larry doing a voice impression." Mom lowers her voice. "But your dad being good at what he did was one hundred percent real."

My mind instantly jumps to Jay's confession yesterday, about how his latest video was all sponsorships and people thirsty for screen time. That even his grandma just wanted to feel famous. This might have worked for my dad, and it obviously works for Jay, and gets him paid, but, God, I hate everything about the idea of not being real, not being myself. If that's what it takes to have a successful channel, selling your soul for the ad revenue, I don't want anything to do with it. Teaching people how to make stenciled burlap candleholders may not get the views, but, damn, at least I can keep my dignity.

I let out another long sigh. "I just wanted Dad to be proud of me, but I can't make stuff up like that. I feel like I let you both down."

"Do you think that going to SCU is the only way Dad would be proud of you? The only way I would be proud of you?" Mom's voice cracks with emotion. "Sweetie, I'm proud of you every day, and I know Dad would be, too. No matter where you go to college or what video you make."

"But that's why you let us come this weekend."

Mom groans. "I was just hopeful that there might be another way we could pay for this, and I latched on to it. I felt terrible about the scholarship, and I feel terrible that I can't provide the money for you. I shouldn't have put that on you, sweetie. I'm sorry you felt so pressured."

There's a thought that has been rolling around in my head for the past couple of days, and I haven't let it take root in my head. But now that I'm talking to Mom, now that I know she won't be mad at me, I quietly let it out. "I could always go to community college for two years and then transfer. I met this guy here who is doing that. He's starting SCU in the fall."

Just saying it out loud makes me feel lighter. Freer. Like I've taken off some huge weighted vest that I've been wearing around all weekend and I can finally move freely. I push myself up from the grass and head off toward the campsite.

"That sounds like a really good idea," Mom says. "We can talk about all the options when you get home. We should have been talking about the options this whole time. For now, please give yourself a break and enjoy the rest of the festival, okay?"

"I'll try." Tears of relief prick my eyes, but I hold them back. "I'm heading back to the tent right now. Jordan is still watching some bands with this friend we made, but I needed a little time alone."

"Get some rest, sweetie. I love you. And Dad loves you, too. Always."

I shove my phone in my pocket, silencing it first, because I can't really deal with any other conversations like that one today, and I try to sort through the tumultuous sea of thoughts in my head as I make my way back to the campsite. It's all too much to process, though, and my brain feels overloaded and foggy. When I open the flap of my tent, which has never looked so comfy, I collapse onto my sleeping bag before I can even zip the tent flap back up all the way.

I didn't imagine myself actually sleeping when I came back here, but once my body hits the air mattress and my head hits the pillow, my eyes close, and I'm asleep before I know what happened.

I have no clue how long I'm out, but an unfamiliar voice right outside my tent jolts me back to consciousness.

"Knock, knock," the voice says.

When I sit up, my head is cloudy, and I'm confused and unsure of where I even am or what year it is. I blink a few times, in a feeble attempt to get my bearings, when I hear the voice again. "Andi? Are you in there?" The voice is definitely speaking in a British accent. This is quite a bizarre dream.

"Uh, yeah?" I reply to the voice.

"Can we come in?" An unfamiliar head peeks through the small opening in my tent flap.

"Who are you?" I sit up on my knees and grab my phone, ready to dial 911 or throw it at someone's head if I need to.

The flap zips all the way down, revealing three skinny white guys with fancy hair and hoodies squatting in front of my tent. I give my head a quick shake, trying to clear the grogginess and make this situation make sense.

"Wait. Are you . . ."

The attractive one in the front sticks his hand out. I figure if he's trying to attack me, he probably wouldn't try to shake my hand first, so I meet his hand and shake it.

"Bernard White," he says.

"Oh my God." I jump up from my crouch, but my head bonks the pole on the side of the tent, so I sit back down again. "You're from the Known. You're the Known."

"In the flesh," Bernard says. "So, are you going to invite us in, or what?"

CHAPTER 12

>>> • <<<

"OH, OF COURSE. COME IN. I MEAN, DO YOU HAVE room?"

It doesn't matter if they have room, because the Known are coming in. All three of them, to my two-person tent. The three members of the headlining band of this entire festival are practically sitting on my lap.

"Do you mind if I ask what this visit is all about?" I'm trying to play it cool, but inside I'm freaking out. I must still be passed out and dreaming, because there's no way this situation makes sense in the real world.

"Well," Bernard says, settling in to Jordan's air mattress, "these fellows Jay and Matthew came backstage for a scheduled interview, and Jay told us you were actually the one who was supposed to be doing the interview, which seemed to throw Matthew off a bit. We tried to get ahold of you, but you didn't answer, so your brother told us where to find you, and here we are."

My mind races to catch up with all this information

he just dropped on me. "Wait. Jay Bankar said I was the one who was supposed to interview you?"

"Yeah," one of the other guys, who I recognize as Theo Abbot, their drummer, says in a British accent that sounds different from Bernard's. "He tricked us a bit, actually. He got us on the golf cart and drove us here straightaway, leaving Matthew behind, saying there was a mix-up, and that it was quite important that you interviewed us. So, here we are."

"He . . . stole you?"

"In a manner of speaking," Theo says. "He dropped us off with our consent, but only after he started driving. Our manager is outside in the cart to drive us back, so we're not completely stolen. He isn't pleased about it, and he has us on a strict timeline, but he knows we love an adventure."

Well, shit. My entire weekend revolved around winning this interview so I could change the course of my YouTube channel, but now that it's here, I'm completely unprepared. Not only did I never finish getting questions ready or set up my camera and lighting, but I'm pretty sure my hair is sticking up in eight directions and I have the imprint of my pillow on my face. I don't even have time to process this Jay stuff. I need to get into video mode, *stat*.

"Well," I say. "I have to admit I'm a little surprised about all of this, but I'm really glad you're all here." My professional voice kicks in as I stick my hand out to each of them. "I'm Andi Kennedy, and if you could just give me a minute . . ." I scramble to find my vlog camera and my ring light and my phone, which somehow got wedged under my pillow. I totally forgot I turned off the volume, and now I have five texts, all from Jordan. The most recent one says, *I'm on my way right now.* Thank God. *HURRYYYYYYY,* I reply.

"Okay," I say, ready to fake it until I make it. I did type up those few questions on a note on my phone in the internet tent, even though I didn't brainstorm any of them with Jordan or come up with new questions they had never been asked before, or any of the other things I assume people who know what they are doing do. God, I don't even know if this is their first time playing at Cabazon. I'm going to ask the worst questions, I just know it. *Get yourself together, Andi. You can do this.*

My attempt to attach my camera to the tripod is clumsy and shaky, and the whole situation slips out of my hands and lands in my open bag. As I dig around to retrieve my rig, my fingers brush against something smooth and cold and rectangular at the side of my duffel. It's much bigger than my camera, and something inside of it clatters around as I pull it out. My box of colored pencils. In the last hour or so before we left for the weekend, I did some panic packing. Tossing things into my bag that I would never use or need, like a coloring book and this box of colored pencils. Of course I never took them out of my bag. Why would I? Why did I think I would?

I stare at the box for a few moments, long enough for Martyn, the third member of the Known, to say, "Andi? Are you okay?" As I look up at him and see his expectant face, something clicks inside of me. Some combination of yesterday's conversation with Jay, today's phone call with Mom, Dad's memory, my jangled nerves over this band's presence in my tent, and my knowledge that this is it, the chance to get that video that would get me views and turn my channel into the thing that could possibly pay for me to go to college with my brother at our parents' alma mater, just like I want to.

"I'm good, Martyn," I say, finally fishing my camera and tripod out of my bag. I turn on the camera, set up my light, and dig around in my bag again, feeling around for the coloring book. "How do you guys feel about arts and crafts?"

>>> • <<<

"This is Andi and this is Bernard, Martyn, and Theo of the Known, who are headlining this year's Cabazon Valley Music and Arts Festival. We're all sitting here in the two-person tent I'm sharing with my brother in the Cabazon campsite on Sunday, the final day of the festival. How are you guys doing today?"

"Fantastic. Thanks for having us," Bernard says. "And

I love what you've done with your tent here. Lovely. Just brilliant."

"Well, I knew you were coming, so I tidied up the place for you."

"Yes," Theo says, giving the side-eye to my pajama top crumpled in the corner of the tent. "I can tell."

"Okay, guys. Normally I'm all about crafting over here on my channel, and it's not every day that one of the world's biggest bands is popping in to my campsite. I didn't bring any crafts with me here to Cabazon, but I did bring this." I hold the coloring book and my box of colored pencils close to the camera. "So, today we're going to do coloring with the Known."

The three members of the Known steal looks at one another from the corners of their eyes, and for a brief moment, I think they're going to tell me to shove it and hop their British arses back on that golf cart as fast as they can. But ultimately Martyn says, "Why the hell not?" and I know they are in.

"Okay, guys, everyone is going to get an inspirational quote to color. You can pick out the colors and really make it your own. Show off your personalities."

"Oh, I love a good inspirational quote," Bernard says. I choose one of the pages at random and rip it out as neatly as possible, holding it up to the camera before passing it across to him.

"Yours says 'enjoy this moment.' I hope you are

enjoying this moment, Bernard. I know I am. Martyn, for you I have 'good vibes,' because you are bringing the good vibes here to this tent right now. And Theo, you get 'go in unexpected directions.' That's appropriate, I think, because getting driven to this campsite on a golf cart by Jay Bankar was probably a pretty unexpected direction for you today."

"Jay was the nicest kidnapper we've ever had," Bernard jokes.

I let out a snort. What story could Jay possibly have told them that would make him seem like the nice guy here? But the camera is rolling, and I'm trying to be a professional, so even though I had every intention of talking shit on Jay on my next video, doing it in front of the Known will only make me look bad, so I bite my tongue.

Instead I focus back on the coloring book, and the only uncolored page left for me to use. "Mine says 'be true to yourself,' which is exactly the reminder I needed today." I show my blank page to the camera. "So, we are going to color while I talk to the Known."

"That sounds brilliant," Bernard says. "Let's do this."

As soon as the coloring begins, the pressure to ask perfect interview questions is lifted, and we just talk. I ask them the craziest thing they've seen backstage at Cabazon, but they don't need to name names. I ask them about LA, what they do when they're there, and to tell me about the best LA show they ever played. I ask them about things they did for fun back in the UK when they were my age, and they turn it around on me and ask me what I do for fun.

We talk about our favorite bands, and I recommend the Gold Parade to them, and they say they'll check out their latest album. They tell me stories about being on the road and the challenges of making music, and they ask me about the challenges of being in school and making videos, and they talk to me like I'm an actual human being.

And the whole time we are working on our coloring pages and holding them up to the camera to show off our progress. Martyn colors outside of the lines, Theo has a green monochromatic color scheme going on, and Bernard uses all the colors of the rainbow.

It's all going to be so great on the video, and my mind races with all the cool things I can do when I edit.

Jordan finally shows up and snaps a few pictures of me interviewing the band, then he has us all huddle into the corner for some group pics and selfies. "Send us those so our manager can post them to our photo stream," Martyn says, and I try not to die. They have literally millions of followers. Then they each sign the three coloring pages. Martyn says, "Why don't you give these away to your followers or something?" and I feel my spirit float right out of my body.

If they actually take the time to post this picture and link to me, I could have thousands more subscribers within an hour. If I can use these signed coloring pages as a giveaway to people who subscribe, having people share for extra entries, who knows what will happen. My pulse pounds as I plan it all out in my head, how I can best take advantage of this incredible, unbelievable opportunity. But even more than that, I notice how my soul feels free. Light. This situation with Jay had brought me down and made me feel bad about myself, but it wasn't until I had the opportunity to do something I was good at, something I loved, that I was lifted back up. I may not be good at judging people these days, but I am damn good at making crafting videos for YouTube.

"Well, Andi," Bernard says, trying to stand up in the tent, but ending up in a hunchback position instead. "Our manager is having a small panic, so it's time for us to run. We have to start getting ready for our set."

"It was a pleasure," Theo says, sticking out his hand.

I shake hands with all of them, and we pile out of the tent into the fresh air.

"Let's get one more group picture before we go," Jordan says, and we all pose in front of the tent, the three members of the Known tossing their arms around me casually like we are best friends from way back.

"Oh, wait! Before you go . . ." I open the back seat of our Highlander until I find yesterday's shorts and pull out the other friendship bracelet I made. The pink one. "You probably don't remember this, but my dad actually interviewed you a long time ago, when your first album came out. His name was Sam Kennedy, and he worked for KPON radio here in LA."

"Oh, I remember Sam," Bernard says, his voice softening. "That was a fun interview. You're his daughter? I'm sorry about your dad."

"But it looks like you're following in his footsteps here." Martyn claps me on my shoulder. "I'm sure he would be proud of you."

My cheeks heat up at these unexpected compliments for both me and my dad. My dad, who did make an impression on this band all these years ago. And me, who maybe did, too.

"Well, this is for you guys," I say, handing the bracelet to Bernard. "From me and my dad. It's pink, like the Cabazon logo. Sorry I only have one. I didn't realize I'd be meeting you guys today or I would have made more."

"I love it," Bernard says. "Thanks."

"Oh, yeah." Theo reaches in his pocket. "Jay gave us this to give to you." He pulls out my other friendship bracelet from yesterday, the green one I tied onto Jay's wrist with extra embroidery floss, and hands it to me. Jay somehow got it untied without cutting it off. Apparently, I don't tie as tightly as he does, since his seems to be welded on to me. "He said he figured you'd want it back."

A weird feeling strikes me as I take the bracelet from Theo. A twist of sadness and regret, and I'm not sure what to do with it, so I shove it all in my pocket with the bracelet. "Thanks. I do."

Then the members of the world-famous, award-winning band the Known all hug me and say goodbye and hop into the golf cart that I didn't even notice. They wave as their manager drives them away, and Jordan and I wave back. As soon as they are out of sight, we look at each other and scream. Loudly.

"Did that seriously just happen?" I jump from foot to foot, finally releasing all the crazy energy that built up inside of me while I pretended like this was all a typical day in the life of Andi Kennedy, interviewing famous bands in my tent and taking selfies like we're all besties.

"It did." Jordan says. "And I have the pictures to prove it." He hands me his phone, and I scroll through the photos he took. Thank God I was able to smooth my crazy tent-nap hair down enough to look decent. And the lighting was on point. Perfect.

"Ooh, this is a good one," I say, showing him a pic he snapped mid-interview. I'm saying something that looks ridiculously intelligent, and the three members of the Known are holding up their coloring pages and laughing with these natural smiles on their faces like this is one time of many that I have made them crack up. "I'm posting this right now."

I AirDrop the picture to my phone, and then I sit down right in front of our tent and get to work editing it and uploading it to my photo stream. "I can't believe this just happened. I can't believe I'm about to post a picture of me with the freaking Known."

"Don't forget to send it to Mom, too," Jordan says. "Her head will explode."

We stay there for a few minutes as I filter and caption and upload and text, continuing to rehash the surreal experience we went through together.

When the initial excitement wears off, Jordan sits next to me in front of the tent, and I rest my head on his shoulder, neither one of us really wanting to bring up what got us here in the first place.

"So, did Jay seriously do that?" I finally say. I'm almost whispering because his campsite is so close. Even though I'm sure he's not there, I don't want to risk him, or Dev, hearing, just in case. Maybe he did stick around after he dropped off the band so he could eavesdrop on me.

Jordan nods. "He actually called me asking where to find you."

It takes a second for my brain to process what he told me. "How did he get your number?" is the first question I manage to form.

"Matthew, I think? I didn't really ask."

"Oh, yeah," I say. "I put you as my emergency contact

on the release I signed. Kinda pointless since you were with me the entire time."

He laughs. "Yeah, and some help I was when you actually did have an emergency."

"So, why did he call you?"

"Do you mean why did he call and not text? Or why did he call me and not you?"

"Both, I guess. None of this really makes sense, honestly."

"I guess he wanted it to be a surprise? And I guess he wanted to make sure I paid attention and heard the phone. It was an urgent situation."

"I'm still having a hard time believing he did this." For the millionth time, I have to shift my mental picture of Jay Bankar. The guy from today, the guy who was ignoring me this morning and whose brother sabotaged my win and who acted like he didn't even care, that guy would never in a million years give up this interview to me.

The other Jay, though. The one I met on the first day and the one I talked to, and kissed, last night? That Jay would do it. He told me the video Jay wasn't him, but then why did he act like that earlier? And why did he change so much now?

"I can't figure this guy out," I say. "Nothing he does makes any sense, and frankly, it's getting annoying."

"Getting? It's been annoying this entire time." Jordan shrugs. "I think you need to talk to him."

I jerk my head toward the Bankar camping spot across the way. "Do you think he's over there?"

"Who knows. He didn't say where he was when he called me, but he was probably driving that golf cart."

I creep across to the Bankar campsite. If I didn't run the risk of tangling with Dev, I would just call out Jay's name or burst through the tarp myself and see if he was back there. No sounds emerge from the other side; I shake my head at Jordan and walk back over to him.

"Nothing," I say.

"So, what are you going to do?" Jordan stands up and stretches himself out.

"No clue," I say, reaching into my pocket to run my fingers over Jay's friendship bracelet. If Jay could manage to keep a consistent personality for more than twelve hours, I could figure this out. But he keeps changing and my impression of him keeps changing and my reaction to him keeps changing, and now my feelings spin around like they're caught in a tornado. "Let's go back to the festival, and maybe we can figure it out on the way."

We walk the long path back to the festival entrance for the final time. The sun is going down, and so are a lot of the campsites. Some setups are already torn down and packed up in cars, while others are in various states of disassembly. The first time we walked this path, on our way to the opening of the festival, the energy was tangible, but now the party is dying. A lone girl in a sundress dances in the middle of one of the camp streets, a red Solo cup dangling loosely from her fingers.

I shove my hands in my back pockets. "If this all works out, maybe I won't have to leave you to fend for yourself next year after all."

Jordan stops in his tracks. "Look, Andi, about that. I'm actually kinda pissed about this."

I cock my head at him. "What? Why?"

"You're my sister, not my babysitter. And I don't need a babysitter, anyway. I'm a legal adult. We're going to college, not preschool."

I reach out for his arm, grabbing on lightly. "Not a babysitter, but . . . you have a lot to worry about, and you're notoriously—" I chew on my lip as I try to figure out the gentlest way to proceed. "Well, I don't want to say irresponsible, but you aren't exactly reliable."

"Well, that's my problem, isn't it?" He shakes his arm free of my grip. "I don't need you to be my personal secretary. You'll have your own life to worry about. And just, like, let me make my own mistakes. Let me fuck up and live with it."

"So you don't want me to go to SCU with you?" I try to keep the hurt out of my voice, but it creeps in there. How could he not want me around?

"Of course I do." He wraps me into his arms, squeezing hard, and I melt into my brother's hug. His chest rises as he pulls in a long breath, and I know he has more to say. "But maybe it would even be good if we split up. Maybe it would be good if we both had a chance to have our own identities."

I stay close against him, tucked into his chest, and I crumple at this suggestion, his words so heavy in my heart. My brother, my twin, doesn't want me around. I suck in a breath and let it out slowly as this confession of his tumbles around in my head. The more I breathe and the more it tumbles, the more it dulls, like a rock on the beach smoothed by the constant beating of the waves.

Hadn't I felt more like myself when he wasn't around? Hadn't it felt like a relief to have something else to focus on besides him?

Wouldn't it be nice to just worry about myself for a little while?

Finally, I pull out of our hug and look up at him, his face that looks so much like mine, his shaved head, his worried eyes, scrunched up as he looks down at me.

"Don't be mad," he says.

"I'm not. And maybe you're right. I don't know. I've just been so scared about how things are going to change and I'm just not ready to do it alone. But maybe I should. Maybe both of us should."

He pats me on my back. "We don't have to make any decisions right now, okay? We're still here. We haven't even graduated yet. We have time to figure things out."

We go back to walking, past the general store and the food trucks, glowing in the late afternoon sun.

"You should decide what to do about Jay, though," Jordan says gently.

"Do you think I should try to find him?"

"I don't know. But this is a pretty big deal, don't you think?"

"It is. But his brother sending strangers out to trip me so I would lose was a big deal, too." I pull my restless hands from my pockets and cross my arms across my chest. "We could just call it even now and move on with our lives."

Jordan scratches the back of his head. "You could, but . . ."

"But what?"

"I know that if I did this for a girl it would be because . . ."

"Because what? Because you'd want something in return? You shouldn't do nice things for girls because you have expectations, Jordan. Relationships don't work that way."

Jordan stops in his tracks. "God, Andi, that's not what I was going to say. Is that really what you think of me?"

"Well, what were you going to say?"

"I was going to say if I did something so huge for a girl, it would be because I was trying to tell her something and I wanted to make sure she heard it."

That turns over in my head, along with my time with Jay last night, as Jordan and I start walking again. "So, you think this is some kind of grand gesture?"

"It would be coming from me. I don't know how this guy operates, though."

I chew on my thumbnail. "Do you think he expects some grand gesture in return? Because I'm not a grand-gesture type of girl, especially after today. And I don't think he deserves one."

Jordan shakes his head. "I doubt it. The thing about a grand gesture is you know there's a possibility it will not have the effect you're going for and it will blow up in your face. But you have to give it a try anyway."

We walk into the festival, and the conversation moves on to other things, but Jay is never far from my thoughts. Jordan and I catch two bands on the smaller stages and then head back to the Outdoor Stage for Run Ahead, one of our favorites, but not before we get our last round of Spice Pie.

"I think we've only eaten pizza all weekend," I say.

"Well, and breakfast burritos," he says.

"Oh, yeah, you're right. The best food groups." We shove pizza in our mouths and say our goodbyes to Spice Pie. "I'm going to miss this so much."

Jordan's phone beeps, and he pulls it out. "Do you mind if Sadie meets up with us?"

I shrug. "Why not?"

As he texts her back with our location, I ask, "What's up with you two, anyway?"

"Nothing," he says, but he can't keep the smile out of his voice.

When Sadie meets up with us, right as Disarm wraps up their mind-blowing set on the Outdoor Stage, Jordan hugs her and kisses her on the cheek. The three of us head off toward the center of the festival grounds, with no real destination in mind. I'm taking in the desert dusk as it settles over the polo fields, the long balloon arches that stretch from one end of the festival to the other, and the twinkling fairy lights that have flickered to life on some of the structures. I wish life always looked this magical.

"So, what happened with you earlier?" Sadie says.

Her question snaps me back to reality. "What do you mean?"

"Jordan took off before with no real explanation, just said that you needed him."

"Wait, Jordan was with you when all this went down?" I look from her to my brother, who smiles back at me. "You left Sadie for me?"

"Of course I did. You needed me."

I throw my arms around his waist and squeeze. "Aww, you really do love me."

I'm joking, but I am honestly touched that Jordan put me before this girl, this very beautiful girl. For once, he didn't let me down.

"See? I can do the right thing on my own," he says, laughing.

The three of us find an open patch of grass to sit, where Jordan and I fill Sadie in on everything that went down, and I show her my pictures of me with the Known. Sadie may not be tuned in to most of the bands here at the festival, but you'd have to be from some other planet to not know the Known. They played on the American Music Awards, the MTV Video Music Awards, and the Grammys, and they have one single, "Chevron," that got megapopular last year and seemed to be on the radio every second for a few months. As I tell her the story, her mouth falls open.

"Jay gave up the interview for you?"

"Well, yeah . . ."

"That's a big deal," she says.

"I know it is, but . . ."

"I mean, would you do that for him?"

That's a good question. Hell, no, I wouldn't. His brother tried to ruin me, and then Jay treated me like he didn't even know me. But she doesn't mean would I do that for him now. She means would I do that for him, for anyone, as a grand gesture. No matter who I was trying to impress, no matter how badly I wanted someone, I can't imagine handing over a huge opportunity like this one to some dude. I need my channel to take off because I need the money. I need college. I need that connection to my dad. There's no way I would give any of that away, especially to someone I didn't even know last weekend.

I wonder what Dev has to say about the fact that Jay gave his interview to me. That would have been a fun conversation to eavesdrop on.

"Ugh," I say as I pull my knees close to my body and hug them. "I need to find him, don't I?"

"I would," Sadie says.

I shake my head. "Nah. I'm not big on second chances."

She looks at my brother, who shrugs and says, "Our dad used to say that."

Sadie wrinkles her forehead. "No disrespect to your dad, but, come on, second chances aren't always bad. It's not like they show some kind of weakness. Sometimes they're about forgiveness. And forgiveness is something that heals you when you offer it to the other person."

"But people don't change," Jordan says. And I can't help but snort because he is the poster child for this fact.

"But sometimes they do, though." Sadie pats him on the leg. "Or sometimes they realize that they really, really fucked up."

I lie back in the grass and look up at the twilight sky. For the first time in as long as I can remember, Jordan actually left a girl to help me out. And not just any girl, one of the most beautiful girls either one of us has ever seen close up. Doesn't that show he can change? And haven't I always forgiven him? Trying to see the best in him, extending that grace, well, it never felt like weakness, just like giving my brother another opportunity to do better. That's not always bad.

"Okay, putting second chances aside," Sadie says, "don't you want to thank him?"

"Or at least hear what he has to say?" Jordan adds.

"Whose side are you on?" I pop back up and jab him in the ribs with my elbow.

"Yours," he says. "I don't want to see you leave here with regrets."

I'm not sure I'll regret leaving here without talking to Jay Bankar again, but I guess I will regret not saying thank you. I'm not completely uncivilized.

"Okay, okay. We were DMing the other night. I guess I can slide back in there and see where he is."

"Never fear, sister," Jordan says. "I have his number."

I look at him quizzically.

"He called me earlier, remember?" He pulls out his phone and scrolls until he finds Jay's number, then he hands me his phone. "Here you go. Text away."

Dang, he solved that problem quickly.

I grab the phone from him and stare at Jay's number on the screen. I take a deep breath before I pull out my own phone and type it in. Then I hover over the text field planning my words carefully. Do I go for funny? Tell him all my feelings now and let him decide? Just throw down some emojis and hope he gets the point?

I finally decide simple is best.

Hey Jay, it's Andi. Where are you right now? Want to meet up?

Then I hit SEND.

I don't want to stress over waiting for an answer, so I shove my phone in my back pocket and say, "So, what's the plan for the rest of the night?" The words are hardly out of my mouth, though, when my pocket starts to vibrate.

"Uh," I say. "Hold on." I pull the phone out. "It's him."

Outdoor Stage. Where are you?

"I don't know how to tell him where to find us. I need a landmark."

Jordan points to a Spice Pie stand about a hundred yards away. "Tell him to meet us over there."

Meet us at Spice Pie by the Outdoor Stage

"Okay, let's go."

The three of us walk over to the Spice Pie stand, and it doesn't escape my notice that Sadie reaches over and grabs my brother's hand. She's the one grabbing for him, not the other way around. Interesting.

I chew on my thumb as we wait for Jay to show up, and I find my head turning at every single person who walks by, even white guys, girls, and older people. I'm losing my damn mind.

"Do you think he'll bring his brother?"

"Not if he knows what's good for him," Jordan says. "That guy is the worst."

"Oh, there he is," Sadie says, and I follow her finger to where she's pointing out into the crowd. Sure enough, there is Jay, with his baseball hat and hoodie on, walking toward us. When he sees us, he tentatively raises a hand in the air. I can see in his face he's nervous, and I'm nervous, too, because I have no idea which Jay is approaching us right now. Is this going to be awesome Jay, who makes me laugh and seems to understand me in ways no one else has been able to? Or is it going to be asshole Jay, who acts more like his brother than anyone should ever act ever?

I raise my hand in a wave back at him, and he smiles. Good sign.

"Hey," Jay says when he gets close enough. He keeps his distance, but even from where he stands, his face and his body language give away how unsure he is.

"Uh, we'll leave you two alone," Jordan whispers in my ear.

"What? No," I say through my teeth. "Stay with me."

"I think it will be better for all of us if we go," Sadie says, patting my arm. "Awkward conversations are never better with an audience."

Before I can object any more, Jordan and Sadie walk off hand in hand. Jerks. Jordan coming through for me was clearly a one-time deal. I bet this was just as much about them getting some alone time as it was leaving me to fend for myself with Jay. They wave to Jay as they pass him, and I can see Jordan say something and Jay say something in return, but I can't hear it or even tell how their mouths moved.

So now it's just the two of us. Me and Jay. And I have no idea what to say to him.

"Um, hi." Yeah, Andi. Way to talk.

"Hi," he says. He shoves his hands in his pockets and looks at the grass.

"So, the Known." When I say it, his head snaps up, eyes full of expectation. "Uh, thanks." Wow, I'm really having a hard time getting actual words out of my mouth.

"How'd it go?" he asks. "I was going to come in with them, but I didn't want to make it weird. Well, any weirder than it was, you know?" He laughs, but it's not very convincing.

I'm shoved in the shoulder by some people trying to get Parmesan cheese topping for their Spice Pie, and a big inhale brings the not-so-fresh scent of day-three porta-potty to my nostrils. Perhaps the space between the pizza line and the bathrooms isn't the best ambiance for important conversations. "Um, can we go for a walk or something?"

"Oh, yeah. Sure," he says. We walk off in the direction of the Outdoor Stage with no real destination. There's a frenetic energy in the air tonight, with the sun setting behind the Ferris wheel on the last night of the festival. It seems louder tonight than it did the other nights, and because of that, Jay and I have to walk closer to be able to hear each other.

"So," I say at the same time he says, "Well." We both laugh nervously and we both fiddle with our hands and we both start to talk again at the same time and we both laugh again.

"You go first," he says finally. "Otherwise we'll never get through this."

I let out a deep breath. "Okay. So, I need you to explain today. All of it."

"Let's sit," he says, waving his hand toward the grass. I cross my legs and sit down, and instead of sitting next to me, like I expect, he sits directly across from me, our knees touching.

"Okay, first of all, I need to apologize to you for earlier. I was a total dick, and I'm so, so sorry," he says.

"Yeah, you were a dick. But you aren't the one who sabotaged me and then filmed it."

He shakes his head. "God, my brother. Are you okay? I'm sorry. I didn't even ask. I've been so freaked out today about everything." He reaches out and touches the bandage on my ankle. "Is it bad?"

I shrug. I've been so high on adrenaline from the Known that my injury has been the furthest thing from my mind. "It's better now."

He seems sincere in his distress, but trusting his sincerity hasn't always been the right move. Can I do it now?

"It's not okay, though, and I feel like such an ass. God, after I spent all this time yesterday telling you that I wasn't like my brother and that the guy you see on my videos isn't really me. And then . . . ugh, I can't apologize enough."

"Well, then, why? Why did today happen? Because all of this made everything you said to me last night a lie."

"I know." He stares off at the horizon for a few seconds, and then he turns back to me. His hands twitch, and he seems to be reaching out to grab mine, but then he sits on them instead. "Okay, so you know last night when my brother came out and wanted to talk to me?"

"You mean when he cockblocked you?"

Jay laughs. "Yeah. That's a better way of putting it."

"Yes, I remember it quite clearly."

"Well, he'd had this whole epiphany. That we were so close to earning back my college money and that not filming at Cabazon was a wasted opportunity. I wasn't lying when I said we weren't going to film here at all—I really just wanted to have fun and relax for the weekend—but he had, like, ten good ideas for us that he'd come up with while watching bands during the day, and he wanted to get us ready to film today. So, I know he came off a little jerky last night, but it was because he was trying to help me."

I cross my arms. "And out of the ten ideas he had, the thing you landed on was having someone injure me so you could film it?" Ugh, this isn't going well.

"No! God, Andi, no. I had no idea he was going to do that. We couldn't agree on anything. I kept thinking about what you told me last night, you know? How this isn't just like acting, that what I do really does affect people. So I couldn't get on board with any of his suggestions for a prank. I kept thinking about what you would think about these pranks, what you would think if you were watching, and I couldn't do any of them. He got so mad at me and told me he would figure something out on his own. He promised me that if I showed up to the scavenger hunt in character, he would take care of everything else. But he swore to me he would leave you out of it, which is the only way I would agree to filming anything." His hands form and release fists over and over. "I knew I shouldn't trust him, but it's so much money. It's college. We needed to do something."

His words hit me at a deep place inside. *It's so much money. It's college.* Understanding of the panic he must have felt sinks down into my stomach.

Jay is quiet for a moment, and he looks around the crowd.

"It killed me to be such a dick this morning, but I thought if I could just get through the scavenger hunt and film the video, I could explain everything and be done with my brother for the rest of the day and—"

"And what, exactly?" I lean back, resting my weight on my hands behind me, putting a little distance between us. "I'd just forgive you after you ignored me? I'd be okay with being part of one of your prank videos?"

"I swear, I had no idea he was going to involve you at all. He was just going to do it to whoever was close to us in the scavenger hunt, and it happened to be you. If Quan had been the next one up, it would have been him." He lets out a humorless laugh. "He gave those people Starbucks gift cards to get in your way, promised them they would be on the video. He always has a pocket full of them just for this reason. Can you believe that? But they weren't supposed to trip you; that was a total accident. I know that's no excuse for any of this, though."

He shakes his head and looks up at the sky for a few moments before looking back at me. "It feels like he pranked me, too, and it feels awful. I'm so done with the videos and being this person. It's not worth it if I'm hurting people." He leans over his knees, getting closer. "It's not worth it if I'm hurting you. You have to believe me, Andi."

From the look on his face, this open, desperate look of regret, I do believe him. I do. This face in front of me is his real face, not his video face. His slouching shoulders and his wrinkled forehead and his open vulnerability would never exist on camera.

But just because I believe him, that doesn't mean I'll forgive him.

"I know I'm asking for a second chance and I don't even deserve it, but, Andi," he says, "I am so sorry."

His apology hangs in the air, floating between us, for several minutes as I try to figure out what to do with it. Finally, I pull the yellow and green friendship bracelet out of my pocket. It rests on my palm, which I hold out between us.

"Prove it."

"What?"

"You said you're done with the channel. You're done being YouTube personality Jay Bankar. But I bet you're going to go home and film another video tomorrow."

He gives me a half-hearted smile. "Well, we never film on Mondays."

"Jay. I'm serious. You've had, like, eighteen personalities since I met you. How am I supposed to believe anything you say at this point?"

"Okay, I'll prove it." He pulls his phone out of his pocket and points it toward me, snapping a picture of me smiling in the Cabazon dusk. "Mind if I post this?" he asks, showing me the picture.

I lean forward to study it. My smile is hesitant. My

eyes are hopeful. My hair looks cute. "The picture is fine," I tell him. "But what are you going to say?"

He smiles as he narrates what his thumbs type up on his phone. "Your boy did a big interview at Cabazon this weekend. Dropped a lot of truth bombs and even made a friendship bracelet. You'll have to check out this amazing girl's channel for the real talk and the friendship bracelet skills. I'll let you know when it's up, but go subscribe to her now so you're the first one to see it." He looks up at me, eyes expectant. "And I'll tag you, of course."

"I don't get it," I say. "You want me to interview you?"

"You already did. Yesterday."

Memories of our time in the craft tent crash into my mind like a wave. Jay confessing the truth about his channel, the truth about Dev, the truth about himself, all as I taught him how to make the sloppy bracelet that's still tied to my wrist.

"You can post it, Andi. Edit it, of course, and cut out all of your stuff. But don't edit out what I said." He takes a deep breath. "I'm done being an asshole on YouTube. I'm done hurting you. It's just not worth it."

"But what if I don't want you on my channel?"

"Oh," he says, looking down.

But I think about what he's doing here, what a huge leap he's making. Giving up this huge thing, this huge part of himself. And, while I won't say he's doing it *for* me, he wants me to be a part of that change. He wants me to be part of this better version of Jay.

"But maybe it could work." I give him an encouraging smile. "Crafting with Jay Bankar. I mean, I got coloring with the Known already. Maybe I could teach beauty guru Sadie Díaz to make custom wreaths or something. Who knows, maybe if those take off, I could even ask the Gold Parade if they want to get together for some macramé or quilting or journal making."

Jay laughs. "Crafting and interviews. Just like your dad."

"Yeah. Just like my dad." And interviews that aren't scripted. Interviews where people share their real feelings, like Jay did with me. Like Jay wants to share with the world.

"Are you sure you want to do this?" I lean over and rest my hand on his knee. "The money?"

"I have to," he says.

Our eyes are locked, and we're smiling at each other, and I feel nothing but how right this is.

"Post it," I say. "Let's do this."

"God, Dev's going to kill me," he says. Then he takes a deep breath and taps SEND on his phone. "And I have no idea what I'm going to do about my parents. Or college. And Mobilocity is sure going to be pissed about being stuck with me as a brand partner now. But, damn, this feels so good."

My mouth falls open slightly as I watch this go down. Jay Bankar is going to let me broadcast his renouncement of his online persona. He's sending me traffic and giving me control of the editing. There will be no fake voice. No chance to take it back.

"But I don't want to be that guy anymore. I want to be the kind of person you'd be proud to be seen with."

Is it possible he really means this? Is it possible this is the real Jay?

But, that would mean giving him another chance, and I don't give second chances. That's what Dad taught me.

Maybe that's why his day is always so bad. Maybe he's trying to send us a message, let us know he was wrong and he doesn't want us to live that way. Maybe Sadie is right, and second chances are about forgiveness, not about weakness.

"Andi, what are you thinking? Say something?"

But I don't say anything. Instead, I lean across the short distance between us, and my lips meet his. I shift so my arms are on either side of him, and the force of my body in his personal space sends him pitching back. His mouth opens to meet mine and we're kissing feverishly. Intensely. I balance on one arm so my other hand can go around his neck and caress the back of his head, weave through his hair.

He moves an arm around my back, and with it he pulls me forward in to him, and on some level I'm aware that

I'm sitting on Jay's lap and we're making out like the world is about to end, but on every other level I don't give a shit because this is amazing.

"Andi," he says when he kisses his way over to my ear. "Are you sure this is okay? I mean, we're—"

"It's so okay. Less talking, more kissing."

"Got it." His breath is hot in my ear and he doesn't move on from that area. He kisses from my ear down my neck and stops at the hollow at my collarbone. I throw my head back a little bit, and without realizing it, my eyes fall open for a second. In that second I see the fairy lights twinkling above us and the festival crowd milling about around us and I'm snapped back into the reality of where we are. I mean, sure, it's dark and all, but still, we're getting a little intense for being all the way out in public. I have to have some standards of behavior here.

I pull away from him slowly and smile. "Well," I say. "Maybe we were getting a little carried away."

He smiles back. "I can think of worse things we could have done."

He runs his fingers through the sides of my hair, then pulls them down so his palms rest on my cheek. "Andi," he says. "I am so sorry. I was such an asshole, and you are so amazing."

"You redeemed yourself. Sorta."

"If you let me, I'll keep trying to redeem myself. As much as I can." He kisses my neck until I can't take the tickling from the lightness of his lips on my skin, and I squirm away, repositioning myself so I'm sitting right in front of his legs and leaning back into his chest. His green and yellow friendship bracelet fell into the grass at some point, so I pick it up, lift his arm, and slide it around his wrist again. "You lost this," I say. "But here it is."

He wraps his arm around the front of me and pulls me in close. "I set it free and it came back to me. That's pretty cool."

"I don't want the festival to be over tonight. I feel like we wasted so much time."

"We did, and that really sucks. But we'll see each other soon. I'm in Pasadena all the time. I'm going out there next weekend, actually."

I squirm around so I can look him in the eye. "Why?"

"My uncle. He owns a restaurant in Old Town. Akbar?

"Oh my God, I love Akbar! My mom takes us there every year for our birthday."

"We film a lot of our videos in the back room there, actually."

I bristle at the thought of his brother. "Well, you can leave Dev at home," I say. "But I'm so glad to know I have some more Jay in my future. And more Akbar."

"Exactly. So when we leave tomorrow, this won't seem like a goodbye. Not for real."

"Especially because I'll be airing your video in about a

week." I give his knee three strong pats. "You'll be hearing from me so much you'll wish we'd never met."

"Now, that? Impossible." He sucks in a little air between his teeth. "So you're really going to do it?"

My eyebrows knit together. "You want me to, right?"

"I really do."

"And I don't think you are going to be my last interview while doing a craft, so I might be bugging you for some connections."

"Bug away. I'd love to help."

He squeezes me as I lean back into him, enjoying our closeness and the feeling of his arms wrapped around me.

We're quiet and still for a few minutes until my phone vibrates with a text.

"It's Jordan."

> *Hope everything is ok. Don't forget the Known go on in 30!*

I show Jay the phone. "We can't miss this. We should head over there."

"Where is your brother? Is he still with Sadie? Let's find them."

I type a reply to my brother asking where he is, and Jay and I head off toward the Main Stage. It seems like the entire festival is gathering to watch the Known, so I have no idea how I'll be able to find them, but it's worth a try.

I check my phone again.

Right behind the soundboard at the Main Stage.
Come find us!

I grab Jay's hand, lacing my fingers through his, then I squeeze tight and lead him through the crowds of people gathering to see the Known. Obviously they're a hugely popular band, but I didn't realize it would literally be tens of thousands of people standing around for their closing set.

Which is why it's even more amazing that Dev Bankar manages to track us down in this teeming sea of humanity.

And, boy, is he mad.

"Jay! What the hell?" He approaches us from the side and grabs Jay by the arm, jerking him to a stop. "I just saw that picture you posted. What the hell is going on?"

"Let go of me," Jay says, wrenching free from his brother's grip. "How did you even find me?"

Dev rolls his eyes, as if the answer is obvious. "I tracked the GPS on your phone."

Jay's mouth curls. "Stalker much?"

"This is because of her, isn't it?" Dev rolls his eyes in my direction, and I back up a step from the sheer force of his annoyance. "I can't believe you're throwing away everything we have for some chick."

"Hey, leave me out of this," I snap, at the same time

Jay says, "This has nothing to do with her." At least we're on the same page.

Dev just shakes his head. "There's no way you're giving up all this money, Jay."

"It was just supposed to pay back my college fund. That's it. And we're pretty much there."

"So that new car you wanted? That trip to Mexico we were planning? You don't want any of that anymore?"

Jay's face flinches slightly, and there's a pause, probably as he mentally says goodbye to all that stuff he was going to buy with his hypothetical money. "It's fine, Dev. I'll get a job. I'll get three jobs. I'm just done doing things this way. This way doesn't work for me anymore. It never did, really."

I expect Dev to start growling from anger, but as he steps closer to Jay, getting right in his face, and my stomach tightens in anticipation of what he's going to do to his brother, I don't see anger at all. I see confusion. And his voice takes on a softness I haven't heard all weekend. "Why? We have so many subscribers, and we get more every day. Our grandma video made that *BuzzFeed* list. Dude, we just won a partnership with Mobilocity. We're trendsetters. Why would you give that up?"

"I don't want to be a trendsetter if it means that I have to be a shitty person. I'm not like you. I don't like getting attention for being a dick."

Dev shakes his head. "I don't get you, man." His voice takes on an unexpected kindness that sounds so out of place coming from Dev Bankar's mouth. "People would kill for what we've managed to build."

"This is your thing, Dev. It's not for me."

"But we've done it all for you. I just wanted to help you."

"I know you think you're doing it for me, but it's hurting me just as much as it's helping. I don't want to live like this anymore."

Looking resigned, Dev sighs. "I don't want you to regret this," he says quietly.

Jay looks his brother straight in the eyes and smiles. "I regret a lot of things I've done recently, but this isn't going to be one of them. We'll talk on the way home, okay?" Then he turns to me and reaches out his hand. "Ready to go, Andi?"

"I'm so ready." I grab his hand and lace our fingers together again. This time he squeezes tightly and smiles down at me, and we make our way into the growing crowd, leaving a confused Dev Bankar behind us. Well, I leave him behind me. Jay will still have to deal with his brother later tonight and for the rest of his life, but from the smile of accomplishment on his face, I have a feeling that the balance of power between the Bankar brothers has shifted just a little bit.

Jay and I finally find the soundboard somewhere in

the middle of the sea of people, and right behind it we see my brother and Sadie, who are totally making out. They aren't two seconds from being horizontal like Jay and I were. But it's pretty obvious they have momentarily forgotten they were in public.

Jay and I join the crowd as the Known take the stage, and as the first notes of their set hit the open air, I pull out my vlog camera to film a little bit, even though we're so far away I can really only get a good shot of the video screens.

"Hey, Cabazon! We're the Known!" When their first song is finished, Bernard holds his mic and walks across the stage with a swagger only rock stars can pull off. "We want to give a shout-out to our new friend, Andi Kennedy. Hope you and Jay are out there making up, love." Then they launch into their next song.

I scream. Jay screams. Jordan and Sadie scream. The people around us scream, even though they have no idea that the shout-out was for us, that one of the biggest bands in the world called out our names on one of the biggest stages in the country.

It's all so surreal, and I want to do whatever I can to remember everything about this night, to freeze this feeling and hang it up in a frame on my wall to remember forever. Turning my vlog camera toward my face, I grab Jay and kiss him, right on film, as the music of the Known vibrates around us.

This moment needs to be captured. This moment with music pulsing through me, turning me inside out and changing my life. This moment where I gave a second chance and a second chance was given to me, and it felt like grace and hope and forgiveness and a lightness I didn't know I needed.

This moment where my dad is with me, always with me, even though he's gone.

And this moment, this night, where the future has been cracked wide open for me, ready for me to run to it with open arms.

ACKNOWLEDGMENTS

This book started as a germ of an idea after my own trips to the Coachella music festival, where, just like Andi and Jordan, I camped, watched a lot of my favorite bands, met some interesting people, and ate a lot of pizza. Since I jotted down those first few ideas, the characters have changed and the story has changed, but what hasn't changed is Andi's love of live music, because it's based on mine. I don't intend to keep writing books about music (and, in fact, I don't even remember writing this book at all—it was just on my hard drive one day, all finished), but music is at the heart of everything I do, so it keeps making its way into my stories.

Swoon Reads, you're the best! Thank you to Jean Feiwel and Lauren Scobell for providing the perfect home for Andi and Jay. Kat Brzozowski, I'm so glad our publishing paths keep crossing. You bring out the best in me, and I truly love working with you. Rachel Diebel, thank you for your insight into my story—this book is better because of you.

Mallory Grigg, your gorgeous cover design made me gasp in delight. Lelia Mander and Celeste Cass, thank you for your attention to every little detail. Publicist Cynthia Lliguichuzhca. What a dream team of publishing rock stars!

To the wonderful, supportive, encouraging group of authors known as the Swoon Squad, thank you for taking me in and cheering me on. I feel so lucky to be in your company. And I'm especially happy to be in the Squad with Shana Silver and Katy Upperman, two talented authors and dear friends who have been by my writing side for every step of this journey.

And, of course, enormous thanks to the Swoon readers for loving Andi and her story! Every single comment I got from you absolutely warmed my heart.

There aren't enough words to thank Elizabeth Briggs. Liz, without you, I would have tossed my laptop out the window and quit writing about seventeen different times. Your gchats of encouragement and constant cheerleading have gotten me through some of my hardest times, and I literally don't know what I would do without you. That's not even hyperbole. I truly don't know. Thank you for believing in me and for being total #authorgoals.

Thank you Kelsey Toney for reading my draft and lending your expertise, both YouTube and otherwise. You are sunshine personified, and your friendship is a gift. And to all of my writing friends: Kathryn Rose, Rachel Searles, Audrey Coulthurst, Alison Miller, Lola

Sharp, Janae Marks, Elodie Nowodazkij, and everyone else in the writing community: you all make this weird, lonely writing life a little easier and a lot more fun.

To my Spalding MFA family, especially my Prague/Berlin and Rome workshop groups, thank you for work-shopping very, very early versions of this story and helping me shape it into what it would become. I don't think I ended up taking Lei'la's suggestion to have Andi check out Jay's butt more, but I definitely never forgot it. You are all a talented and incredible group of writers and my favorite people to travel with.

Thank you to my gal pal gang, Claire, Erin, and Tameka, for being such supportive friends. How lucky I am to have you in my life. #galpals #virgosvslibras #ijustreallyloveani-mals #ifyourenotextrayouarentalive #wehavefruit

Amol Bankar, you will probably never see this and you probably wouldn't remember me anyway, but I used your last name, so, even though we haven't spoken since 1994, I have to say thank you. As a teenager, I was convinced we would reunite and get married. Obviously neither of those things happened, but I still think of you every time I hear "Layla" by Eric Clapton. Jay's hotness and charm are both based on you.

To all my students, from CHS to CVMS to EMHS to VPHS: Every single one of you has touched my life. Some of you might find your names in my books, but all of you will find your essence, because every single one of you has inspired me. Nothing but love to all of you. Stay safe and make good choices.

To my husband: thank you for putting up with me always being on my laptop and constantly having a deadline. I know it isn't easy, and I know the house is a mess, but your support as I follow my dreams means more than you'll ever know.

And to my sweet little boys, absolute lights of my life, how lucky I am to be your mom and watch you grow. I love you all the time, every day, no matter what.